MURDER
IN A SEASIDE TOWN

The death of a bookseller gives Irish detectives a novel problem

DAVID PEARSON

Paperback edition published by

The Book Folks

London, 2021

ISBN 978-1-913516-87-1

www.thebookfolks.com

For Joan, with thanks for your support and encouragement.

Chapter One

Sergeant Séan Mulholland was asleep in his bungalow on the Sky Road near Clifden in the west of Ireland. Although it was late September, the Garda station that Mulholland managed had been busier than usual for the time of year. He was supposed to keep the station open until eight o'clock, but this evening, things had dragged on a bit, and he hadn't locked up until well after half past.

As was his habit, once the station was closed for the night, he made his way up the town and settled down beside the turf fire in Cusheen's Bar, where he drank three pints of Guinness quite slowly while reading the paper from cover to cover. Then he drove home.

At shortly after three o'clock in the morning, the sound of his mobile phone – a rather old-fashioned Nokia device which suited him well – jangling on the bedside locker took eight rings to break into his slumber. He eventually reached out and picked up the phone, fumbling for the little green button to answer it. He didn't recognise the number on the display, other than it was a local one.

"Hello," he said rather hoarsely.

"Séan, Séan – is that you?"

"Of course, it is. Who's calling, please?" Mulholland said, fearing a prank call.

"It's Bridget, Séan, from the post office."

Bridget O'Toole was the postmistress who lived above the little post office on Market Street in Clifden with her daughter.

"Oh, right, Bridget. What time is it?"

"It's quarter past three, Séan. I'm calling because there's something going on down here in the town."

"Oh, God, right. What's the problem, Bridget?" Mulholland said, shaking off his sleepiness and starting to focus.

"Well, I'm after hearing a gun go off in the house next door – or maybe the one beside it. And then I heard a door slam, and someone running off down the street. Can you come in, Séan? I'm scared stiff."

"Are you sure, Bridget? You weren't just having a bad dream, now, were you?"

"No, no. I don't sleep that well. I know what I heard," Bridget said rather indignantly.

"Right. Stay where you are then. Don't go near the place or anything. I'll be down in about fifteen minutes."

Mulholland dressed in his Garda uniform as quickly as he could. He raked a comb through his shock of thick grey hair, and had a quick look around to make sure he hadn't left too many lights on, and stepped out into the cold autumnal morning.

He sat into his old Saab, which started reluctantly, as if it too did not appreciate being called into service at this ungodly hour.

"I must leave the car into Ferris and get him to fit a new battery before the winter sets in," he said to himself, "I don't want to get stuck somewhere unable to get her started."

The drive down into the town took a mere eight minutes. He met no other traffic, and as he pulled up outside the post office, he turned the front wheels towards the kerb to stop the car running off down the hill. The handbrake wasn't very effective.

Bridget O'Toole, dressed in a long flannel nightdress, a heavy plaid dressing gown and a hairnet, opened the door that led up to her flat over the premises, and stepped out onto the footpath.

"God, Séan, I hope I was mistaken. Are you going to have a look?"

Mulholland wasn't thrilled to hear that Bridget, having had time to consider the likelihood of a gun being discharged in the middle of the night in Clifden, was now having second thoughts. But as he had already arrived, he thought he should investigate, if for no other reason than to put the postmistress's mind at rest.

"I am, of course. Now you step back in there out of the cold, Bridget. I'll go down and have a poke around, and I'll come and tell you if I find anything."

"Right so. Be careful, now," she said, retreating back into her hallway.

Mulholland placed the peaked cap he had been holding on his head, and set off down the street. He had no weapon of any kind on his person, but he didn't feel the need. This was beginning to look more like a wild goose chase with every passing moment.

He went to the next-door property on the terrace that housed the post office. It looked to be secure. There were no lights on inside it, but that was hardly surprising at this hour of the morning. When he got to the second house in the row, he saw that the door was slightly ajar. Again, there were no lights on inside the place, but the door should not have been open like that. He knocked three times, but got no response – nor was there any sound from within the building.

Mulholland pushed the door open gently and peeked inside. He had had the good sense to bring a torch with him, and he shone the bright white light all around the hallway, observing that nothing appeared to be out of place. Stepping inside, he went to the room on the right of the hall, opening the door and repeating his scan using the torch. Again, all seemed peaceful. At the back of the house, there was a downstair cloakroom and then the kitchen spread out across the back with a window looking onto a small paved courtyard that had a rotating clothes line, a small garden bench and a fuel bunker. The kitchen was neat and tidy, with some crockery on the draining board beside the sink where it had been left to dry.

Mulholland then turned his attention to the upstairs. The stairs itself was carpeted, and although quite steep, didn't creak as he made his way gingerly up to the first floor. He called out, "Hello – is there anyone home. It's the police."

There was no response.

When he reached the upstairs landing, he noted that the door to the bathroom stood open, and a quick glance into the room told him that it was empty. He then had two other doors to choose from – presumably, bedrooms. He knocked on the one directly in front of him, stating once again that it was the police, but there was no response. He gingerly opened the door, and shone his torch through the gap, before entering the room and turning on the light. It was a single bedroom with all the expected furnishings. A bed, nicely made up with what looked like fresh bedlinen, a small dresser with a mirror, and a narrow wardrobe. A bedside locker completed the inventory. The curtains were open, but when Mulholland checked the wardrobe and under the bed, there was no sign of anyone.

The second bedroom was very different.

Mulholland repeated his approach, but when he got the door open and turned on the light, he was met with a scene which he swore afterwards would never leave him as long as he lived. This room contained a double bed, and there, lying on it, was a woman with shoulder-length blonde hair, dressed in a flimsy nightgown that stopped well above her knees. But the entire centre portion of her torso was just a bloody mess, and much of what had been her stomach and lungs were now sprayed around her in a random, chaotic pattern.

"Dear God in heaven," Mulholland said out loud.

Although he was a seasoned Garda with many years' service, he had rarely come across such a gruesome scene. He had attended road traffic accidents that could be pretty unpleasant, but he had never been up close with a murder victim such as this one, and the experience shook him to the core.

He stood back out on the landing, keen to put some distance between the dreadful mess in the bedroom and himself, as his training slowly kicked in. There was no point in trying to establish if the woman was still breathing – it was clear that life had left her some time ago.

Firstly, he got his phone out and took a few pictures of the scene with the rudimentary camera. This would have the dual effect of recording the time, and capturing the horror before him. Then, a little reluctantly because of the hour, he called Senior Inspector Maureen Lyons on her mobile phone.

* * *

Lyons was a detective in her early forties who had climbed her way up through the ranks of the Gardaí on her merits. She had chalked up a number of victories over the criminal classes in the Galway area, starting when she was just a rookie with the apprehension of an armed bank robber outside the TSB on Eyre Square. She was known to be a tough woman, who wasn't afraid to tackle the lowest form of thug, a characteristic that had caused her to be shot at more than once, not to mention being left for dead in a filthy bog hole overnight by a ruthless killer. But she was resilient, and was not inclined to let these types get the better of her; as a result, she had earned a healthy respect in the force.

Lyons was in a deep sleep when her phone started to tinkle and vibrate on the nightstand beside the double bed that she shared with Detective Superintendent Mick Hays in their house in Salthill, close to Galway's city centre. It was an unusual arrangement, and one that was not encouraged by management in the Garda Síochána, but they had been a couple for a number of years now, and despite the initial misgivings of Chief Superintendent Finbarr Plunkett, it had worked out well for all concerned.

Lyons could see from the phone that her caller was, much to her surprise, Séan Mulholland.

"This must be serious," she said softly to herself. Hays was still fast asleep.

"Yes, Séan, what is it?" she said, cupping her hand around the mouthpiece of the telephone to deaden the sound, and trying not to show her vexation at being woken at such an hour.

"God, Maureen, it's terrible. I'm out here in Clifden in a house two doors down from the post office. There's a woman here in the bedroom with her middle shot out. It's a terrible mess. I'm not the better of it, I can tell you."

"I presume the woman is dead, Séan?"

"She is that. I got a call from Bridget O'Toole about three quarters of an hour ago. She said she heard a gunshot and someone running away, so I came in to investigate, and that's when I found her."

"OK, Séan. Are you all right?"

"Well, no, not really, but I'll do. There's no sign of the perpetrator or the weapon here in any case. What do you want me to do?"

"Can you secure the scene for us, Séan, and get a couple of your men out to make sure no one goes into the place, no matter who they are. I'll get the pathologist and forensics out as soon as I can. What time is it now?"

"'tis just coming up to four o'clock, Maureen."

"Right. Do you know the identity of the victim?"

"No, I don't. I might have seen her around and about, but I don't know her name – Bridget will be able to tell me," Mulholland said.

"OK. Well, I'd better get to work making arrangements. I'll see you in a bit."

"Right, Maureen, see you soon."

Chapter Two

Lyons grabbed the clothes that she had taken off a few hours previously, and with her phone welded to her ear, she began to dress hurriedly. She called the Garda station at Mill Street, and instructed the night man on the front desk to get busy notifying Dr Julian Dodd, the pathologist attached to the Galway force, and Sinéad Loughran, the forensic team leader, of the tragedy in Clifden and requesting their presence at the scene as soon as possible.

Next, she called Detective Sergeant Sally Fahy who was to all intents and purposes her right-hand colleague, and alerted her to the events.

"I know it's crazy, Sally, but can you meet me out there asap? I'll need your help. I'm on my way now."

"Yes, sure, boss. I'll be right behind you."

Disturbed by all the commotion, Mick Hays stirred in the bed and asked Lyons what was going on.

"There's been a serious incident out in Clifden. Some woman has got herself shot, or so Séan says. I'm on my way out there now."

"Do you need me?" Hays said, hoping against hope that the response would be in the negative.

"No, you're grand. Anyway, you need your beauty sleep! I'll call you later when I know what's going on."

Hays turned over gratefully and dozed off again.

Lyons left the house, ensuring that she had her mobile phone, a few pairs of vinyl gloves and some evidence bags with her, and hopped into her Volvo for the journey out west.

* * *

When Séan Mulholland got back outside the house, he was met by Bridget O'Toole, still clad in her dressing gown and hairnet.

"What's happened, Séan? Is the woman all right?"

"No, Bridget, I'm afraid not. Don't go in there now – it's not a pretty sight. It looks as if she's been shot at close range. And I'm afraid she's dead."

"Oh, God in heaven! That's terrible. Will I get Father Murphy?"

"Do you know the woman, Bridget? Is she a Catholic?"

"Sure, of course she is. Did you not see her at Mass every Sunday?"

"No, Bridget. I usually go on Saturday evening. It's quieter then. But what's the woman's name? Who is she?"

"Her name is Ann Sweeney. She's lived in that little house for around three years with her son, Dónal. But he's away in college now, so he's not here anymore during term time."

"Is she not married or what?" Mulholland said.

"No, she was. Married to some blighter over the far side of Galway – Ballinasloe, I think. It didn't end well. I think he used to knock her about a bit. She never said much about him. But I probably have his PRSI number in the post office. Would you like me to have a look?" the postmistress said, keen to get further involved in the mystery.

"Ah, no, you're grand. We'll find him quick enough if we need him. Did the woman have many visitors, Bridget?" Mulholland went on.

"Well, I'm not one to pry into other people's business, but she did. A few different men that called at odd hours, like late into the night."

"I see. And how long would these visitors stay, Bridget?"

"Sure, how would I know. I didn't keep watch. But I'd say maybe an hour or thereabouts."

"And tell me, Bridget, did you recognise any of these late-night callers at all? Were any of them local?"

"Ah, now, Séan, I never got that good a look at them. They were in and out that fast, and there's no street lamp outside the house. But I'll say this, they were well dressed and drove nice cars."

"I don't suppose you remember anything about the cars – the colour or make or even the numbers?"

"Not a bit of it. Sure, I wouldn't know one car from another, and I don't go around making notes of people's numbers, Séan, what do you take me for? Anyway, I'd better get back indoors. It's a bit chilly out here and me in my night clothes. Come on in after if you like to chat some more. I'll not be asleep."

"Right, so. And best leave the priest for now. I have instructions not to let anyone near the place till the crowd from the city get here."

Bridget turned and walked back up to the door of her own house, and went inside.

Mulholland rather reluctantly called his closest ally in the small force that manned the Garda station in Clifden. Jim Dolan was a quiet sort, but thorough, and always ready to help out where possible. He was married and had two children, and lived close to the Garda station out on the Galway road on the edge of the town.

"Jim, it's me," Mulholland said, having woken his colleague from his night's sleep.

"Hello, Sarge. What's up?"

Mulholland related the events of the past hour to Dolan and asked him to come down to the house and get a couple of the uniformed lads out too, to secure the scene while they waited for the team from Galway to arrive.

* * *

By five o'clock, the main street in Clifden was a busy place. A sombre black Mercedes van had arrived out from Galway University Hospital ready to receive the remains of Ann Sweeney when Dr Dodd had completed his initial examination. Two marked squad cars were parked at the side of the road, and Sinéad Loughran's Toyota Land Cruiser, along with Lyons' Volvo and Sally Fahy's Ford, completed the mini traffic jam.

Lyons, having carefully placed blue plastic overshoes on her feet, ascended the stairs and stood at the door to the bedroom where Dr Julian Dodd was examining the poor woman. He looked up from his gruesome work when he saw the senior inspector.

"Shotgun, by the look of it. Quite a spread of the pellets from it too. I'd say the killer probably stood in the doorway or maybe even a bit further back to discharge the weapon. Sinéad may get some more detail from the bedhead for you. I'll get the remains back into Galway. Shall we say two o'clock?"

"And what time would you estimate she was killed, Doctor?"

"I think the post office woman said she heard a shot at around 3:00 a.m., didn't she?"

"Yes. Would you concur with that?"

"Yes, I'd say that's about right." Dodd and Lyons left the house, making room for the two men from the morgue to come inside with their thick plastic body bag and manoeuvre the lifeless form of Ann Sweeney into it, and down the stairs. As soon as the body was clear, Loughran and her assistant, dressed in white paper scene-of-crime suits, got started looking for evidence.

Back outside, Lyons said to her colleagues, "Why don't we retire to the Garda station here and leave Sinéad to get on with it? When the hour gets decent, can you organise a door-to-door with a couple of the local Gardaí, Sally? And see if there's any CCTV anywhere that might have caught the killer making off."

Chapter Three

By mid-morning, Lyons' organisational skills had set a lot of things in train. Inspector Eamon Flynn had been despatched to University College Galway to inform Dónal of the death of his mother. He would take a family liaison officer with him who would stay with the poor lad and try to console him, although that would not be easy.

The remains of Ann Sweeney had been removed to Galway, in preparation for Dr Dodd's post-mortem in the early afternoon. Mulholland, who had been the first to arrive on the scene, would need to be in attendance to confirm that the body he found in the bedroom was one and the same as that about to be examined.

Sally Fahy had taken two uniformed Gardaí from the Clifden station and was out and about knocking on doors to see if anyone had seen or heard anything during the night that might help the Gardaí identify the perpetrator.

"Séan," Lyons said to Mulholland who was just about to have his third cup of tea of the morning, "when you've finished that, can we go and speak to Bridget O'Toole. She should be up and about again by now. Then we had better get into Galway for the PM."

"Right. I'll leave my tea. I'm not in the humour for it in any case. C'mon and we'll go and see what Bridget has to say."

* * *

The post office had more than the usual number of customers that morning, and the air was filled with whispers and intrigue about what had taken place overnight. Lyons and Mulholland waited patiently for a lull in the traffic, and then asked Bridget if she could lock the door for a few minutes while they had a chat.

The postmistress put a well-used sign up in the glass door advising would-be callers that normal service would be resumed in fifteen minutes, and the three of them retired to the parlour at the back of the building where Bridget offered tea which the two Gardaí declined.

"Bridget – you don't mind if I call you Bridget, do you?" Lyons said, opening the discussion.

"No, of course not, that's what everyone calls me," the woman said, wringing her hands with the tension of the affair, sitting on the edge of her seat.

"Could I ask you to go over again what exactly you heard and saw during the night, Bridget?" Lyons said. "You'll need to come down to the station later to make a formal statement, but if you could just tell us while it's fresh in your mind, it could help."

Bridget went on to describe what she had witnessed, albeit remotely, following the same lines as the story she had told Sergeant Mulholland when she called him at home.

"And what do you know of Ann Sweeney, Bridget?" Lyons asked.

"Not a whole lot, Inspector. She had a part-time job at the library a few mornings a week. She received some social welfare payments here which she collected in cash on a Friday. Oh God, has anyone told Dónal, the poor chap?"

"Yes, don't worry. That's all in hand, Bridget. Go on," Mulholland said.

"Well, there's not a lot more to tell. She kept herself to herself mainly. Quite a private person, she was."

"Do you know anything about her ex-husband, Bridget?"

"Just that he is from Ballinasloe. I think he has a business there of some kind, but don't ask me what. Some that met him say he was a bit rough. Not like herself at all."

"Did he ever come calling?" Lyons said.

"Sure, how would I know?" Bridget said, somewhat indignantly.

"Well, living almost next door to the woman, I thought you might have seen him coming and going occasionally, that's all," Lyons said.

"No, I never did, and I wouldn't know him even if I had seen him."

Lyons looked at Mulholland a little puzzled by the logic of the woman.

"Did Mrs Sweeney have a car, Bridget?" Mulholland asked.

"She did. Not much of a one, mind. I think it was one of those little Toyotas. It'll be out on the street in front of her house."

"Is there anything more you can tell us at all about Mrs Sweeney, and the way she lived out here, Bridget? This doesn't look to me like a random killing, so there must be more to it," Lyons said.

"'tis dreadful, Inspector. We never had the likes of it here in the town. Everyone is scared half to death in case whoever it was comes back. I'll not sleep so well ever again."

"I don't think you should worry, Bridget. It looks like she was specifically targeted, but as to why, well that remains a mystery. Thanks for your help in any case. If you'd like to drop into the station later on, we can write down what you've told us," Mulholland said.

Back outside, Lyons said to Mulholland, "What do you think, Séan? Does she know more than she's letting on?"

"Not a bit of it. I've known that woman for over thirty years, Maureen. She'd have no reason to hold anything back."

But Lyons wasn't quite so sure.

They walked back down the street and passed the library on their way back to the Garda station. There was a handwritten sign stuck to the door of the premises advising people that the facility was closed due to a bereavement.

"Who runs the library, Séan?" Lyons asked.

"That's Angela McCabe. She's the head librarian. She lives a bit out the road, close to Ballyconneely."

"We'll need to speak to her too. Maybe tomorrow when things have settled a bit. Now, you and I had better get going into town for the post-mortem."

* * *

Séan Mulholland got into Lyons' Volvo and the two of them set off towards Recess where their journey would take them on past Maam Cross, Oughterard, Moycullen and on into the city. It was a bright autumn day, and the heathland looked very picturesque with the purple heather now well in bloom and the backdrop of the Twelve Bens framing the scene.

"So, tell me, Séan, how are you managing these days?" Lyons said by way of making conversation.

"Ah, not so bad. My arthritis plays up a bit when it gets damp, but apart from that, I'm grand. But I'll tell you, Maureen, this to-do has fair shook me up. What I saw this morning in that woman's house will stay with me for the rest of my life. In all my years of service in the Gardaí, I've never seen the like."

"I know what you mean. It was a particularly vicious murder, and I've seen a few. Have you any ideas about it at all, no matter how far-fetched?" Lyons said.

"I haven't. And to be honest, I'm not sure if I want to be dealing with this kind of thing at all. Being a Garda in Clifden never prepared me for this. Maybe it's time I hung up my boots."

"Not at all, Séan. There's plenty of life left in you yet. And what would you do if you retired in any case?"

"I'd enjoy a bit of fishing, and the house could do with some attention. It's got very dowdy over the past few years. Nothing a coat of paint wouldn't fix, but it needs doing."

"God, I don't know, Séan, there's only so many mackerel you can eat. Mick brings home dozens of those things when he's been out in the boat, and they don't half stink, and the bloody scales get everywhere!"

The two of them laughed out loud.

Chapter Four

It was nearly one o'clock when Lyons and Mulholland reached Galway.

"Would you go a bit of lunch, Séan?" Lyons asked.

"God, I would. Have we time?"

"Sure. Let's go to the Imperial. They have a good carvery there, and we can park outside."

At the hotel, Mulholland tucked into a full plate of roast beef, roast potatoes, mash, turnips and plenty of gravy, while Lyons settled for a more modest seafood salad. When the sergeant had cleaned his plate, he went back for a thick wedge of apple pie and custard while Lyons just had a coffee to complete the meal.

When they arrived at the mortuary at the back of Galway University Hospital, Dr Julian Dodd was already togged out in a long green rubber apron, cream vinyl gloves and a blue paper hat.

"Good afternoon, Inspector, Sergeant."

"Hello, Doctor," the two said in unison.

As he pulled back the plain white sheet that was covering what was left of Ann Sweeney, he said to Mulholland, "Can I ask you to confirm that this is the person you saw at the house in Clifden this morning?"

"Yes, that's her, poor woman."

"Very good. Then we shall proceed."

One of the doctor's two assistants carrying a stainless-steel tray of ghastly instruments moved in close to where Dodd was now leaning over the corpse. He started speaking for the benefit of the microphone that was suspended over the gurney.

"A woman, estimated age mid to late forties. In reasonably good condition, apart from the obvious. Approximately one hundred and sixty-five centimetres in height, and weighing fifty-four kilograms when she was complete – that's eight and a half stone in old money, Sergeant," the doctor said. He continued with his gruesome task, removing the major organs and passing them to the other assistant who took them away to be weighed and preserved.

Mulholland excused himself and went outside. The whole process was making him ill.

After thirty minutes or so, Dodd stood back from the body and removed his gloves.

"What can you tell us then, Doctor?" Lyons said.

"Quite an interesting specimen you have brought me, Inspector. She was obviously shot at close range with a shotgun. Sinéad has some evidence relating to the weapon. She says it was a 20-bore shotgun. Quite unusual. But Mrs Sweeney has had a bit of a tough time before she was killed too. Nothing very recent, but she's broken a couple of ribs some time ago, and she had a fracture to her left arm at some stage too. Maybe she fell from a horse or something."

"Hmm, maybe."

"There's no sign of recent sexual activity. And her last meal was several hours before death. Pasta of some kind, I'd wager. No alcohol in the system, so she was sober. Oh, and she appears to have lost two front teeth a while back as well – there are implants in number 23 and 24 on the lower jaw."

"Anything else of interest, Doctor?"

"No, that's it for now. We will recover the rest of the shotgun pellets from the body and keep them safely for you."

"Thanks!" Lyons said, somewhat ironically.

On the journey back to Clifden, it wasn't long before the gentle undulation of Lyons' Volvo across the boggy road and the heat inside the car sent Mulholland to sleep. Lyons didn't mind one bit – she was tired herself, but she was not inclined to doze off whilst driving.

Lyons would have liked to go around by the coast road through Roundstone and Ballyconneely, but time was not on her side. She needed to get back to the scene of the crime, and see what the others had managed to find out about the tragic events of the previous night.

* * *

Inspector Eamon Flynn had asked Mary Costelloe to accompany him to University College Galway where they would break the sad news of the lad's mother's death to him, and hopefully get some insight into her lifestyle.

The Student Information Office was positioned just off Alumni Plaza at the rear of the main campus where it bordered the River Corrib in a building called Áras Uí Chathail. Although it was modern and therefore comprised largely of concrete and glass, the end wall had been faced with natural stone which helped greatly to soften the appearance of the place. Flynn parked his car and the two of them got out and went into the building.

It took the helpful and friendly girl a few minutes of research on her trusty computer to establish the likely whereabouts of Dónal Sweeney. It transpired that Dónal was in the second year of a degree in Business and Spanish. According to his timetable, he should be finishing a lecture in the J.E. Cairnes School of Business, theatre K3 on the second floor.

"He'll be finished in about ten minutes, Inspector. That should give you time to find the place," she said and went on to sketch out the route on a pre-printed map of the campus and handing it to Flynn.

When they arrived at the appointed location, the lecture hall was starting to disgorge the students noisily into the corridor. Flynn managed to engage one or two of them as they hurried away, and Mary Costelloe did the same. After a number of attempts, they spoke to a young woman who knew Dónal.

"Thank heavens for that. I was beginning to think he was an illusion," Flynn said, smiling at the young redhead. "Was he in the lecture with you?" he said.

"Not likely. Dónal doesn't really do lectures. He studies at his own gaff most of the time," she said.

"Do you know where we might find him then?" Costelloe asked.

"Probably in his pit, he's not exactly an early riser!"

"And where's that, exactly?" Flynn asked becoming a little impatient with the matter.

"He lives in a house share up on Moyola Park. It's not far. I think it's number 23. I was at a party there last month, it was massive."

"Thanks, we'll try him there then. Thanks for your help," Costelloe said.

When the two of them got back into the car, Flynn put 23 Moyola Park into the sat nav which duly informed him that it was four minutes away by car. He followed the direction provided until the device announced, "You have arrived at your destination."

The house was in the middle of a modern terrace of similar properties that looked as if they had been built in the 1970s or 80s. What may at one time have been front gardens were now tarred over, presumably to minimise maintenance. There were three different-coloured wheelie bins and a rather tired-looking Toyota Yaris displaying the

N-plates that new drivers are obliged to show for two years following a successful driving test.

"Looks about right," Flynn said, getting out of the car. "I hope we don't disturb his beauty sleep!"

They knocked on the half-glazed front door and waited. They could hear noise coming from inside, but no one appeared at the door. Flynn thumped three times very firmly on the badly peeling painted frame which looked as if it might give way at any moment.

After another few moments, a shape appeared in the frosted glass, and the door was opened by a young man in a T-shirt and shorts with just a pair of odd socks on his feet.

"We don't want any. Go away," the lad said gruffly, but he wasn't quick enough to prevent Flynn getting his foot into the door jamb to prevent it from being slammed in their faces.

"Police," Flynn said, holding up his warrant card. "We need to speak to Dónal Sweeney."

The occupant stood back and held the door open.

"Sorry," he said, "I was asleep. I think Dónal is upstairs, but he might not be on his own."

"That's fine. Maybe you could tell him we need to speak to him," Mary Costelloe said.

"Oh, yes, right. You can wait in here," he said, indicating a room to the left of the door.

Chapter Five

Flynn and Costelloe entered the room which measured about four metres by five. The largest piece of furniture was a huge pair of loudspeakers, mated to a separates hi-fi system which Flynn felt could probably be heard all down the street if played at full blast. In front of the system, a semi-circle of chairs in various states of disrepair stood, and there was a low coffee table off to the side where overflowing ashtrays and empty beer cans almost completely covered the top surface. The air in the room was fetid with a pronounced smell of stale cigarette smoke, beer and a hint of weed for good measure. Neither Flynn nor Costelloe wanted to sit down, so they remained standing, taking in the contents of the room.

Sensing what Mary Costelloe was thinking, Flynn said, "Let's not make a fuss. He'll have enough to deal with when he hears the news."

"Yes, I guess you're right."

They heard heavy footsteps descending the stairs, and a young man came into the room. He was stocky, with a lot of brown hair sticking up everywhere, dressed in a twill dressing gown from which pyjama bottoms protruded above his bare feet.

"I'm Dónal, you were looking for me," he said in a husky voice.

"Yes, Dónal. Would you like to sit down?"

"Oh, OK," the lad said warily, taking the seat furthest away from where the two Gardaí were standing.

"Dónal, can you confirm that Mrs Ann Sweeney is your mother, and that she lives in Clifden a few doors down from the post office?" Flynn said.

"Yes, that's right. Why? Is there something wrong?"

"I'm afraid we have some very bad news, Dónal. Gardaí were called to her property at around three o'clock this morning to attend an incident. I'm afraid your mother had been fatally wounded. She didn't survive."

"No! That's not possible. I was only talking to her yesterday. She was fine. There must be some mistake," Dónal said. He had gone very pale, and looked as if he might faint.

"Can I get you a glass of water, Dónal?" Mary Costelloe said.

"What happened? How did she die?" Dónal asked, ignoring the offer of a drink.

"I'm afraid she was shot, Dónal. We're going to have to ask you to make a formal identification, but she was known in the town, and the woman from the post office has confirmed that it is your mother. In any case, she was found in the bedroom of her own house."

No one said anything for a few minutes, allowing the terrible news to sink in.

"But who? I mean have you caught whoever it was? God, did she suffer?"

"No, Dónal, it would have been instant. She probably didn't know anything about it. And our investigations are just getting started. We have no idea who the perpetrator is as yet."

Some colour was returning to the young man's face as he processed the information. He had tears in his eyes, but he was handling it well, given the sudden and tragic nature of the news.

"Why don't we go to the kitchen and get a cup of tea, Dónal. We need to ask you a few questions about your family."

Dónal said nothing, but got up slowly. Flynn led the way to the back of the house where the kitchen was to be found. It was pretty messy, but Mary Costelloe soon found the kettle, some tea bags, a few mugs and even some milk that was still relatively fresh, and in no time, she had a brew prepared.

"Have some sugar in your tea, Dónal, it will help with the shock."

"It's fine. I don't take sugar, but thanks."

After a few minutes of contemplative silence, Flynn began to gently probe Dónal Sweeney about his mother.

"When did you last see you mother, Dónal?"

"The weekend before last. I got the bus out to Clifden, and we went for a drive out as far as Leenaun and had tea in that nice little cafe there. It was a lovely day," Dónal said, and started to weep silently.

"And did your mother seem OK? She wasn't worried about anything in particular, or anyone?"

"No. She was in good form. Cheerful. Relaxed. We had a great time. I stayed over and got the bus back on Sunday. I used to live there until I went to college, you know."

"And she didn't discuss anything at all that was bothering her?" Flynn asked again.

"No, not a thing."

"What did your mother do? Like, how did she earn money for bills and so on?" Costelloe said.

"She worked at the library. She has a great interest in books. Especially old books. She has collected quite a few over the years. The house is full of them. It was only a few mornings a week, but my dad sends her money too, and I got work in the summer in one of the hotels out there and helped out a bit as well. She isn't really into money as long as she has enough to get by."

"So, is she on good terms with Mr Sweeney?"

"She is now – now that they're not living together. He can be very awkward. He's a bit of a bully. Especially if he has drink on, which he has most of the time. But if you don't have to live with him, he's OK. He pays my college fees and gives me an allowance for rent and food and stuff. He's not all bad."

"What does he do for work?"

"He's a builder, well, sort of. He does one-off houses and big renovations, that sort of thing. And he has a few properties too that pay rent."

"So, he's pretty well off then?" Costelloe said.

"I guess."

"Does he have another woman in his life that you know of?" Flynn said.

"No, at least I don't think so. I haven't been to his place for quite a while, but I think he's living on his own. Why don't you ask him?"

"We will, Dónal. Maybe you could give me his address and contact details."

"Yes, sure. But you don't think he could have had anything to do with what happened, do you?" Dónal said, looking at Flynn.

"Probably not, but we have to investigate everything for now, however unlikely."

Flynn didn't want to spook the young man, but was thinking to himself that in these cases it was very often the spouse that was to blame.

"Mary here can stay with you if you like, Dónal. She is a trained family liaison officer, and she can help you over the next few days. There will be some arrangements to be made, and I'm afraid we're going to have to ask you to come in and formally identify your mother. Maybe tomorrow morning?"

"I'll be fine, don't worry. But if someone could collect me in the morning – I don't know where to go."

"Yes of course. Would ten o'clock be suitable?" Costelloe said.

"Yes, that would be fine, thanks."

"Well, if you could just get us your father's details, we'll be on our way. We're very sorry for your loss, Dónal. It's very sad."

Dónal Sweeney got up and found a piece of paper and a pen and wrote down the address for CS Construction, his father Conan's building company in Ballinasloe.

The two Gardaí then got up and departed, leaving Dónal to his sadness and the memories of his dear mother.

Chapter Six

Mulholland woke with a start when Lyons pulled the car up a little sharply outside Clifden Garda station.

"God, I'm sorry, Maureen, I must have dozed off for a few minutes."

"Ah, you're grand, Séan. I'm tired myself. Let's get in and see what the others have found."

Once inside, Lyons called the team around.

"Well, what have we got then?" she said hopefully.

Jim Dolan spoke for the group. "Very little, Inspector. No one, apart from Bridget, heard anything during the night. There's no CCTV worth talking about. Ferris has a camera down at the garage at the corner, but it's trained on the pumps and the shop, so it didn't catch anything if our man did go down that way. That's it, I'm afraid."

"Aw c'mon, folks. There must be something out there. Did you call to every premises? What about around the back of her house – did anyone look there?"

"Yes, boss. There's just a very small garden – no side gate or anything, and no way out. It backs directly onto the hill, and the back door is still locked from inside."

Lyons was at a bit of a loss.

"OK. Well let's see who has a licensed 20-bore shotgun in the area. Séan, have you got the register?"

"Yes, of course. It's in the back office, and it's all up to date."

"Right, well, dig out a list and then Jim can go out and inspect them – there can't be too many of those. You know what you're looking for – any that have been recently fired – and collect a sample cartridge from each one as well, label them carefully, and bring them back for comparison. OK?"

"Yes, boss."

"I'm going back up to her house now that the forensic team have finished. I want to have a good snoop around. We have to try and find a motive for this, then maybe we'll get somewhere. Sally, will you track down the person in charge of the library? Find out as much as you can about the deceased. Spend some time with her work colleagues. See what you can get."

"Right, boss," Fahy said.

"There's only Mrs McCabe that runs the library. She used to have another woman working with her, but the council cut back the funding about two years ago. Ever since, it's just been Angela and Mrs Sweeney, but to be honest, I don't think they were exactly run off their feet," Mulholland said.

"Right. Well, when Sally and I have finished, make sure the house is properly secured, Séan. We'll get back into Galway then. In the meantime, if anything at all comes to light, I want to be informed immediately. And keep an ear out for any gossip around the town. The grapevine is our friend in these situations."

* * *

Lyons made her way back to the house where Ann Sweeney had so tragically lost her life. She ducked under the blue and white Garda tape and opened the door with the Yale key that had been removed by the Gardaí earlier.

The house was single-fronted, with a sitting room of sorts immediately to the right of the hall door. Lyons donned vinyl gloves, and gently opened the door. The room was tastefully decorated in quite a modern style. Three of the walls were painted in a muted pale grey emulsion, with the chimney breast which housed a wrought iron Victorian fire surround, painted in contrasting aquamarine. The carpet was quite fresh. Plain and sandy in colour, it showed little sign of wear. On both sides of the chimney, shelves had been installed from floor to ceiling, and each was tightly packed with books. On the opposite wall, another bookcase had been constructed, again from floor to ceiling, and it too housed dozens and dozens of books, leaving just enough room for a two-seater sofa and a single easy chair to complete the furniture in the room. The single window, which looked out onto the street, had net curtains and more substantial plain drapes suspended on a pole above the window casing. The general feeling in the place was that of slightly cramped comfort.

Lyons browsed the shelves. She noticed that the books had been carefully arranged, almost as if they were in a library. Paperbacks, of which there were a couple of hundred, were sorted alphabetically by the author's surname. The lower three shelves to the left side of the fireplace, and hence out of view of the window, housed hardback publications, many of which appeared to be quite old. Lyons knelt down and took out a random title and opened it.

The book was titled *Good-Bye to All That* by Robert Graves, and it was signed by the man himself on the fly leaf. It was in excellent condition, with no foxing and it was nicely bound in green and brown with gold lettering on the spine. Lyons had no clue of the book's value, but she had a feeling that it might be worth a bit.

The next book she took out was *The Talented Mr Ripley* by Patricia Highsmith, and Lyons noted that it too was a first edition, but in this case, it bore no signature. This book was in less good condition. There were some small tears in the dust jacket, and obvious browning to the edges of the pages, but it was still very much intact.

Lyons continued to browse the shelves, focusing her attention on the hardbacks. After twenty minutes or so, she took out her pocketbook and made a note of ten of the titles she had perused, along with which of them were signed, and their general condition.

The room at the back of the house was a kitchen-diner, and like the front room was in generally good condition. The appliances were quite new, and the room was clean and in good order, but held little of interest to Lyons, so she soon made her way upstairs.

The house had originally had three bedrooms, the smallest of which would have struggled to contain a single bed. Perhaps it was intended for a cot. But this room, like the front room beneath, had been converted for book storage. Shelves had been installed, and again dozens of books had been arranged neatly and carefully in alphabetical order by author. With all the shelves fully occupied, more books were stashed in cardboard boxes, making it difficult to move around. One of the boxes had been upset, and had spilled its contents out onto the bare wooden floorboards.

Lyons glanced at the books that were uncharacteristically untidy, and saw that once again they were old hardbacks dating from the middle of the twentieth century and earlier. She noticed several well-known titles such as *Animal Farm* and *Nineteen Eighty-Four* among those scattered around. It came as no surprise to her that these, too, were first editions.

By this time, the tiredness of the very long day that she had put in was getting to her, so she decided to leave the house and go back to the Garda station, collect Sally Fahy and head back to the city.

Before they left, she asked Séan Mulholland if a computer had been found at Ann Sweeney's house.

"Yes, I believe so. I think young Loughran took it with her. It was one of those portable jobs, a notebook or a laptop or whatever you call them," Mulholland said.

"Thanks. Right, well we're off now. I'll call you tomorrow, Séan, to get the results of the shotgun inspection. All the best for now," Lyons said.

* * *

"Sally, do you know anything about old books?" Lyons said as they drove back along the bog road towards Recess.

"'fraid not, boss. Why do you ask?"

"It's just the dead woman seems to have a massive load of books in her house, and some of them are pretty old. A lot of the old ones are first editions too. I wonder if they are worth anything?"

"Search me. I barely have time to read a few pages on my Kindle at night to send me off to sleep. But we could contact the University. I'm sure they have someone there that knows about old books."

"Yeah, some dotty old professor in a bow tie and a tweed jacket, no doubt. But that's a good idea. Follow it up tomorrow for me, will you? You never know, you might get lucky!" Lyons said.

"Thanks a bunch!" and they both laughed.

Chapter Seven

The following morning, as soon as Lyons got into work, she summoned the team for a briefing.

"Right, folks, there's a lot to do today. We need to move this along before the trail goes cold. Sally, can you go back out to Clifden and talk to the library woman, what's her name? McCabe, yes that's it, Angela McCabe. See what she can tell us about the deceased, you know the drill. Oh, and keep Séan in the loop, I want to keep him closely involved."

"OK, boss. And while I'm out there, I can check on the gun register too and see if that has turned up anything. What about your idea to contact the University about the books?"

"That'll keep, or I might give it a go later if there's time," Lyons said.

"Eamon, you seem to be specialising in house calls. Can you get over to Ballinasloe and see if you can locate the woman's husband. He is some kind of builder, it seems, and a bit rough too by all accounts. See if he owns a shotgun and get a look at it if he does, and of course check out his license and where he keeps it. If it's a 20-bore, lift it and bring it in."

"Right, boss," Flynn said.

"Mary, will you take the son into the morgue for an identification. Chat him up a bit, see if he comes up with anything useful. Oh, and get a set of his fingerprints for elimination out at the house too."

"What are you going to do, boss?" Flynn asked, direct and to the point as usual.

"I'm going to hook up with Sinéad Loughran, see if there's anything on the woman's PC that could be useful, and anything else Sinéad may have found at the house. OK. Let's get to it. Meet back here at five then, unless you're caught up with something important, in which case, phone in."

* * *

It took Inspector Eamon Flynn forty minutes to drive from Galway's Mill Street Garda station to the outskirts of Ballinasloe. He had elected to bring a uniformed Garda with him for two reasons. Firstly, he wanted someone to look up CS Construction, and get directions to its premises in Ballinasloe, and secondly, he wanted to show a bit of strength in case Mr Sweeney turned out to be a bit rougher than anticipated. You never could tell in these situations.

The young Garda had no trouble getting a fix on CS Construction's yard, and programmed the Eircode into Flynn's sat nav, giving them turn-by-turn directions to the place. Flynn turned off the M6 onto the R446 as directed by the device, and drove up along Brackernagh until the sat nav informed him that his destination was on the left. He pulled up in front of two enormous solid metal gates, with the only sign of the company's name in small writing on the letter box attached to the adjacent wall.

The young Garda hopped out and opened the gates, allowing Flynn to drive into the expansive yard. The area was just what you would expect for a builder's premises. A pile of rusting scaffolding was neatly stacked in equally rusty iron frames at one side, while a rather tired-looking mechanical digger with a cracked front windscreen and an equally dishevelled-looking dumper were parked beside each other on the other side. The office, which was centrally situated, was comprised of a long portacabin arrangement, which looked as if it was three individual units joined together, and parked directly outside the nearest one stood a shiny two-year-old Mercedes E220.

"Looks like we're in luck," Flynn said as he re-joined his colleague.

They entered the first of the buildings, and found a man they assumed to be Conan Sweeney seated at a desk inside. Sweeney certainly looked a bit rough. He was probably around 180cm in height, although it was difficult to be accurate because he was seated, definitely overweight, with a round ruddy face and a thin covering of streaky grey hair, arranged in a comb-over in an attempt to disguise advancing baldness.

Flynn introduced himself and his colleague, and established that the man was indeed Conan Sweeney.

"I suppose you've come about the robbery," Sweeney said.

"What robbery would that be, Mr Sweeney?" Flynn said.

"What robbery!" Sweeney said to another man seated at a nearby desk who felt obliged to smirk weakly at his boss's humour. "That's a good one, Guard. The robbery over at the site near Ballywalter, of course."

"No, actually, that's not why we are here, Mr Sweeney. That matter will be dealt with by the local Gardaí from Ballinasloe. We are from Galway. I wonder if there is somewhere private we could have a few words?" Flynn said.

Sweeney looked at the only other occupant of the makeshift office, who got up from his seat and left the three of them to themselves.

"Right, so what ails you?" Sweeney said.

Flynn, although uninvited, sat down on the chair facing Conan Sweeney at his desk.

"Mr Sweeney, can you confirm that you are married to an Ann Sweeney who lives in a house on Market Street in Clifden, and that you have a son, Dónal, attending UCG?"

Any hint of humour had now left Sweeney's face.

"Yes, that's right. But we're not together any more. She left me about three years ago. Why do you ask?"

"I'm very sorry to have to inform you, Mr Sweeney, but there has been a serious incident at your wife's house. A shotgun was discharged in the early hours of yesterday, and I'm afraid your wife was mortally wounded."

"You're kidding, right?" Sweeney said, trying to smile a little.

"I'm afraid not, Mr Sweeney. Identity has been confirmed. It's Mrs Sweeney all right."

Sweeney said nothing. He reached into a drawer in his desk and took out a crystal tumbler and a half full bottle of Irish whiskey. He poured a generous measure into the glass, and drank hungrily from it, draining the amber liquid in one go.

"Jesus! What happened? Is Dónal OK?" Sweeney said in a raised voice.

"Dónal is fine. He wasn't at home. He was at that place in Moyola Park. And as to what happened, we don't know yet. All we can be sure of is that at around 3:00 a.m. the woman who runs the post office near Mrs Sweeney's house heard a gunshot, and when we went to investigate, we found Ann dead in her bed."

"Christ! But how? Who would do such a thing? I know we didn't get on anymore, but Ann is a gentle woman. She'd never hurt a fly. Who could have done such a terrible thing?" Sweeney said, and poured another measure of spirit into his glass.

"When did you last see your wife, Mr Sweeney?" Flynn asked.

"Let's see, it would have been at Dónal's birthday party last year. He was eighteen so we all went out for a meal and I gave him that little car as a birthday present. It was a bit tense, to be honest, but we made some kind of a fist of it."

"May I ask you why Ann left you, Mr Sweeney?"

"Ah, ye know. We just didn't get along any more. Always fighting and bickering. And she didn't like the company I was keeping either, and I was getting fed up with her and her bloody books. It's all she can think of, so it was for the best. I still support her, and the lad of course."

"Can I ask if you own a shotgun, Mr Sweeney?"

Sweeney looked Flynn straight in the eye.

"Now, just hold on a minute. You don't think I had anything to do with this, do you? That's ridiculous. I know I said we didn't get along, but I had no reason to harm my wife, and I'm not happy with your implication, Guard!"

"It's Inspector, Mr Sweeney, and I'm not implying anything. I just asked if you own a shotgun, that's all. Do you?"

"Yes, I do as it happens. All properly licensed and locked up like it should be. I sometimes go shooting birds with it. There's a farmer near my house that lets a few of us shoot on his land."

Flynn looked at the young Garda who was still standing by the door and nodded slightly.

The young man said, "Perhaps we could have a look at the gun, Mr Sweeney, whenever it's convenient for you?"

"Bloody cheek. But, yes, I suppose so. I have nothing to hide."

The young Garda noted down Sweeney's home address and made an appointment to visit the house at seven o'clock that evening to inspect the gun and associated paperwork.

"Thanks, Mr Sweeney, that will be all for now," Flynn said, getting up to leave. As he approached the door of the office, he turned and said, "Just one more thing, Mr Sweeney, where were you the night before last?"

"Asleep in my bed, and before you ask, alone. Where any decent man should be. Now if that's all?"

When Flynn and his colleague were driving away, Flynn said, "Get one of the locals to check up Sweeney's gun and license, will you? What did you think?"

"Yes, no problem. I dunno. He has no alibi, and you know what they say about husbands and wives. But he seemed genuinely shocked at the news," the young man said.

"Hmm, yes I agree. It might be no harm for us to have a good look at his business empire. It doesn't feel terribly prosperous from what we saw at the yard. Did you note the number of his car?"

"Yes, I have it here," the young Garda said.

"Right. We'll check the CCTV cameras out at the start of the N59 as well just in case. There won't be much traffic on it at that hour. Send me his reg on WhatsApp. I'll get John O'Connor to look into it," Flynn said.

Chapter Eight

Detective Sergeant Sally Fahy enjoyed the drive from Galway to Clifden. The weather was pleasant, if not glorious, but the scenery made up for the slightly overcast day. Once past Oughterard, Fahy decided to go into Clifden via Roundstone. She loved the view from the road along by the coast, with the blue-green Atlantic Ocean rolling in against the beaches and the rocks, and the screaming of the seabirds overhead.

When she got out beyond Roundstone village, just as the road straightens out beyond the Catholic church, she spotted Garda Mary Fallon in the car park of the small Garda station where Pascal Brosnan and herself tended to the needs of the community. She pulled her car into the car park in front of the small whitewashed building.

"Hi, Mary," Fahy said, getting out of her car.

"Oh, hello, Sergeant, what brings you out this way?"

"I'm on my way into Clifden to interview the woman that runs the library there in connection with Ann Sweeney's murder. Don't suppose there's a cup of coffee going, is there? I'm parched after the drive."

"Sure. Come on in. We may even have a biscuit or two somewhere," the blonde officer said, gesturing towards the door of the building.

Once inside, Mary Fallon set about making refreshments for them both.

"Is Pascal around today, Mary?" Fahy said.

"He's gone over as far as Tadgh Deasy's garage. He says there's a funny noise coming from the squad car, and he wants to have it seen to."

"Oh, right. The car is quite new, though, isn't it?" Fahy said.

"Yes, it is, but it gets a fair hammering all around here on the boggy roads. I don't think it's anything too serious. Pascal likes to keep an eye on Deasy anyway. You know what he's like."

"Yes, I do. So, is there any gossip around the village about Mrs Sweeney then?" Fahy said.

"Pascal was down in O'Dowd's last night having a pint, and he said there was a lot of chatter going on about it. People are very shocked, and a bit scared too. He said there was some talk of things 'not being right' out at the library in Clifden, but nothing specific."

Mary sat down, putting the two mugs of coffee on the table and a saucer with three chocolate biscuits.

"Thanks, just what I needed. Were there any more details?"

"No, at least I don't think so, but you'd need to speak to Pascal about it. I wasn't there."

"Oh, OK. Maybe I'll drop in on the way back," Fahy said, enjoying the excuse to take the same route coming back that would take her around by Ballyconneely coming from Clifden.

"Anyway, how are things going between you two?" Fahy asked.

"What do you mean, Sergeant?"

"Off the record, Mary. Everyone knows that you two could be an item. We're all hoping!"

"God, is it that obvious? To be honest, he's proving a bit tricky to snag. He's convinced romantic involvement between two serving officers is doomed to failure. You haven't any ideas, I suppose?"

"What – with my track record? I'm a right one to ask, but have you tried food?"

"Food? What do you mean?" Fallon asked.

"C'mon Mary, you're a smart girl. Cook the man a slap-up meal out at yours. Don't hold back – fillet steak, chips, followed by apple pie with lots of cream. If that doesn't do it, nothing will! And don't forget a slight hint of nice perfume. You'll never get rid of him!"

The two women laughed.

"You think that would work?"

"I'd put money on it. Anyway, you've nothing to lose, except a week's wages on the steak," Fahy said, "and if you throw enough wine into him, he won't be able to drive home."

"God, stop! You're awful!" Fallon said grinning widely.

"Anyway, I'd better get going. Thanks for the coffee. I'll drop in on my way back and see Pascal. See you later."

* * *

Angela McCabe was a woman in her fifties, immaculately turned out in a grey two-piece suit, the skirt of which stopped just above the knee. The jacket covered a pale lemon sateen blouse with a revere, and her fair hair, going a little grey at the roots, was neat and fashionably short without looking boyish.

"Well, Sergeant, how can I help you today?" the woman said in a nondescript accent tending towards posh, as she sat behind the modern desk in the back office of Clifden's library which remained closed to the public.

"Firstly, I'm very sorry for your loss. It must have come as a terrible shock to you. Had you known Ann long?"

"Yes, of course, it's a dreadful tragedy. I worked with Ann for nearly three years now. She started here on a voluntary basis, but as soon as we discovered her very extensive knowledge of books, we managed to persuade the council to create a part-time position, and she became a member of staff. I don't know how we are going to manage without her. I suppose I'll just have to look for a replacement, but it won't be easy."

"Do you know anyone who might have had any reason to harm Mrs Sweeney, Angela?"

"No, of course not. Ann was very well liked by the locals. She was able to advise everyone who came in on books and authors that would suit their taste. She was very popular."

"Did you socialize with her at all?"

"Not really. We very seldom went for a drink in the evening if there was a special occasion. But Ann worked mornings mostly, so once she left at one o'clock, her time was her own," the librarian said.

"Do you know if she had a man in her life?" Fahy said.

"I have no idea, Sergeant. Ann was quite a private person. She didn't discuss her private life at work."

Fahy recognised that she was having a hard time penetrating this woman's cool demeanour. She wished Lyons was with her. She would know how to open her up. She tried another tack.

"Do you keep any valuable books here at the library, Angela?"

"No, not at all. We take what we are given by Libraries Ireland, mostly from their stock in Galway. We have a lot of books about Irish literature and well-known Irish writers, and then quite a big fiction section with all sorts. After that it's biographies, history, travel, sci-fi and so on. Oh, and we have quite a large children's section too. The stock is refreshed every quarter, and we can get books to order for people, but there's nothing particularly valuable here, although in a way all books are valuable, don't you think?"

"Yes, I suppose they are. But what about first editions and rare books? Do you have any of those?" Fahy said.

Angela McCabe gave a short laugh, sitting back in her chair.

"Oh, no. You'll need to scour the charity shops in the city if that's what you're after, or maybe some of the specialist shops that deal in antiquarian literature. You'll not find anything like that here."

Fahy was running out of questions fast, and it was frustrating her.

"What about donations of books? Do you ever get those?"

"Yes, we do. When some of the old-timers pass on, and their relatives from Dublin, or further afield, are clearing out the house, they sometimes leave us a few boxes of stuff. That was one of Ann's jobs. She used to go through all that and catalogue it. She'd put anything of interest on the shelves and get rid of the rest."

"And how would she dispose of what was left over?"

"Search me. As long as it wasn't cluttering up the place, I didn't ask. I presume it went to charity in some form or another."

Fahy brought the interview to an end at that point. She felt very frustrated that she had discovered so little about Ann Sweeney from her employer. She wasn't looking forward to telling Lyons about it.

Chapter Nine

"Hi, Sinéad, it's Maureen. Just wondering if you've finished with Ann Sweeney's laptop? We could do with it over here to explore. John is itching to get his hands on it."

"Oh, right. Well, we didn't find anything significant anyway. Mostly Mrs Sweeney's prints and a few others which I guess will turn out to be her son's. We didn't turn it on – that's John's job. I'll drop it over now if you like?"

"Yeah, if you don't mind. Thanks. Oh, and bring a coffee, will ya?"

"Sure! See you in ten."

A few minutes later Sinéad Loughran bounced into Lyons' office juggling the laptop and a small tray with two takeaway coffees.

"Hi, Sinéad. Thanks for the coffee. You're a lifesaver."

"No problem. So how is it going?"

"It's not. Eamon is out interviewing the husband, but I'm not too hopeful. Sally is out in Clifden talking to the woman's employer. Maybe that will yield something. But other than that, so far, it's a complete mystery. Oh, there is one thing though. Ann Sweeney appears to have had a small collection of what may well be quite valuable first editions. But I'm no expert. I'm going to contact the University later and see what we can discover about them."

Lyons' phone rang.

"Lyons," she said.

"Hi. It's me. Listen, could you pop up for a few minutes?"

It was Superintendent Mick Hays on the phone.

"I'm just with Sinéad at the moment. Is it urgent?"

"'fraid so. Now would be good."

"OK. I'm on my way."

"Sorry, Sinéad, that was Mick. I've been summoned on high. And it sounds ominous. I'll catch you later," Lyons said, getting up and grabbing her jacket from the back of the chair.

She knocked on the door and went into Hays' office. He had a visitor.

"Come in, Inspector. Let me introduce Inspector Wallace. He's from Dublin – the Fraud Squad."

Wallace stood up and extended his hand which Lyons shook. He was a thin man, immaculately dressed in a charcoal grey suit, pale blue shirt and expensive silk tie. His hair was very well groomed, and his tanned complexion hinted at a recent foreign holiday – or perhaps a visit to the spray tanning booth. Lyons wasn't sure which. They all sat down.

"Inspector Wallace, would you like to explain to Senior Inspector Lyons why you are here?" Hays said.

"Thanks, Superintendent. I understand you are investigating the death of a Mrs Ann Sweeney, Inspector."

"Yes, that's right. She was killed in her home a couple of nights ago. Nasty business."

"I'm afraid I'm going to have to ask you to, eh, how shall we say, 'suspend' your enquiries for the moment. Mrs Sweeney was known to us, and is, or was, a key component of an extensive investigation that we have been involved in for the last eighteen months. It's at a delicate stage, and we don't want to spoil all the hard work that's been put in to date. We're closing in on a very significant gang of fraudsters," Wallace said.

Lyons looked at Hays, who just shrugged. But he was apprehensive, and not a little concerned about what might happen next.

"Inspector Wallace, are you in a hurry today?" Lyons asked.

"Not particularly. I need to get back to Dublin later. Why? What have you in mind?"

"Come with me then," Lyons said, standing up. "Will you excuse us, Superintendent?"

"Yes, of course. Carry on."

Lyons led a very puzzled Inspector Wallace out of the station to her car. She blipped the central locking, and asked Wallace to sit in it.

When she had started the car and was driving out of the yard, Wallace said, "Where are we going, Inspector?"

"What's your first name, Inspector?"

"Paul, why?"

"Well, Paul, just so we don't get off on the wrong foot, I outrank you, so I'm Senior Inspector Lyons and you're Paul. OK?"

Wallace shifted a little uncomfortably in his seat.

"Senior Inspector isn't really an official rank, is it?" Wallace said.

"You'd need to take that up with the Commissioner, Paul. I can assure you, I have earned my rank, and I get paid more than you do, so that's official enough for me."

Wallace said nothing. He wasn't used to this kind of treatment. He had expected to walk into Mill Street, speak to a senior officer and take complete control of the situation. He hadn't reckoned on meeting Maureen Lyons.

Rather than lock horns with the woman, he repeated his earlier question.

"Where are we going, Inspector?"

"You'll see. Don't worry. I'm not kidnapping you."

Lyons drove to the rear of Galway University Hospital and parked outside the mortuary. She got out of the car without saying anything more, and Wallace had no choice but to follow her. This wasn't going the way he had imagined. He was somewhat at a loss as to how to proceed.

Inside the mortuary, Lyons met one of Dr Dodd's assistants.

"Hi. Could I ask you to bring out Mrs Sweeney for me?"

"Yes, sure. Just wait here."

The two detectives stood in silence waiting for Mrs Sweeney to arrive. After a few minutes, the familiar form of a prone corpse was wheeled into view, covered in a white cotton sheet. Lyons nodded to the girl who had been steering the trolley, and she pulled the sheet away, revealing the badly damaged remains of Ann Sweeney.

Wallace instinctively looked away and put his hand to his mouth. He dashed across to a stainless-steel sink, and was violently sick. When he had recovered his composure, he made his way back to where Lyons was standing.

"Let's get out of here," he mumbled, afraid that his digestive system would erupt again.

Outside, it was clear that the man was not happy.

"What kind of a stunt do you call that?" he said grimly to Lyons.

"That was no stunt, Inspector. You see, while you're sitting in your office chair twiddling with your spreadsheets and accounts up in Dublin, me and my team are out dealing with the true horrors of crime. I've worked several murder cases. I've been shot at. I've been kidnapped and thrown into a bog hole and left to die, and still, I go in pursuit of those that slaughter our fellow citizens. So don't talk to me about 'stunts', and don't tell me to stop doing my job. Now, I think we're finished here. I'll drive you back to Mill Street and you can get back to

Dublin to your nice warm office and comfy chair, and try and forget what you saw in there."

Lyons turned on her heels and got back into her car. She was fuming.

* * *

"Hi, Mick. It's me. Listen, you might be getting a bit of heat from Dublin over Inspector Clouseau. I took him around to get a first-hand look at the remains of Ann Sweeney. I don't think he was too impressed," Lyons said.

"Oh, Christ, I thought you had that look in your eye. Did he survive?"

"Yes, but his breakfast didn't. I'd say he'll be making a complaint."

"Ah, don't worry. I know the man that he reports to quite well. He's a decent bloke. I'll give him a call and head it off. But do you not think it might be better to make peace with them? They may have information that could help you find the killer."

"Maybe. It's just he got right up my nose, cheeky bugger. Do you think I should apologise to him?"

"I'll leave that up to you, Maureen. Do what you think is best. How are you getting on with the case anyway?" Hays said.

"We're not. Nothing. Nada. Except that we know she was big into old books. I'm going across to the University at some point to see if I can get anything there."

"Should I phone ahead to warn them?" Hays said, smirking.

"Feck off, Superintendent. But thanks. Catch you later."

"Bye."

Chapter Ten

When Lyons had finished the call with Hays, she went in search of Sinéad Loughran. She found her pouring over Ann Sweeney's laptop with John O'Connor.

"Hi, guys. Anything?" she said, leaning over so that she could see the screen.

"Well, John here has been able to get into it, at least. He's a genius!" Loughran said.

"Shh, don't let on – he's our best kept secret."

"This is a spreadsheet that I found on the hard drive," O'Connor said, slightly embarrassed by the two women's banter about him.

"It looks like a catalogue of the books she had in her house. There are a few hundred rows, and some of them are highlighted in green, and there's some kind of code number against those ones. There are some estimated values on a separate sheet too against some of the ISBN numbers," O'Connor said.

"What are ISBN numbers?" Lyons said.

"International Standard Book Number. It's a derivation of a system created by a professor in Trinity College, Dublin in 1965. It was originally called Standard Book Number, but when the Brits adopted it a few years later, they changed it to 'International'. It's a unique number given to every book that is published," O'Connor said.

"And who makes up the numbers?" Lyons said.

"They are managed by agents. I think it's Nielsen that allocate them for the UK and Ireland, but I'm not sure."

"Oh, OK. And do all these books have them?"

"No. Many of them are too old, so they are catalogued by publisher, publication date and author. There's a lot of first editions here. You can tell that when the copyright date is the same as the print date," O'Connor said.

"What's the total value of the lot?" Lyons asked.

"Let's see. This is only an approximation, but it looks like a few hundred thousand at least, maybe more."

"Wow! Tell you what, John. Will you keep digging? Pick a few titles from the spreadsheet and do some research on them individually. Find out anything you can about them. Dig deep. Sinéad, can you organise to go out to Clifden and collect all the books and bring them in. We can't have that value of stuff just lying around where anyone could lift it. And can I get a copy of the spreadsheet printed out, John? I'm going to go across to the University later and talk to someone over there who knows about books."

"Right, boss. I'll get that organised straight away," Sinéad Loughran said.

* * *

Lyons telephoned University College Galway, and got through to the library. After a few false starts, she spoke to a Miranda Tregaron, who was in charge of special collections at the establishment. Lyons explained that she was interested in meeting to talk about a collection of books, some of which appeared to be first editions, and arranged an appointment with the woman for the following afternoon. By that time, Sinéad Loughran would have brought Ann Sweeney's books back to town, and

Lyons could bring one or two of the ones she deemed to be rarer with her to the meeting.

When she finished the call, the next one she took was from Séan Mulholland.

"Hi, Maureen. It's Séan. Look, there's been a bit of an incident out here in Clifden. You know Ann Sweeney's house?" he said.

"Yes, of course. What's up?"

"Well, it seems to have been broken into during the night. There's no sign of forced entry, but the place is a right mess. Books thrown around all over the place, furniture turned over, drawers emptied out on the floor. You know the kind of thing."

"Crikey! Right, well don't leave the place unguarded. Sinéad Loughran is on her way out to collect the books in any case. She can give the place the once over while she's there. I don't suppose anyone heard or saw anything?"

"Bridget says she thought she heard some disturbance in the night. She hasn't been sleeping well since the murder. But she was too scared to go and investigate on her own, and she didn't want to call me out in case it was just cats or something," Mulholland said.

"Terrific. Still, I suppose you can't blame her."

"Will you be coming out yourself, Maureen?"

"No, not this time. I'm pretty tied up here with the investigation. But be sure to send in a report. I hope you took a few photos, Séan?"

"Oh, I did of course. I'll print them out for you and give them to Sinéad."

"Right. And ask her to ring me when she's had a look around, will you?" "Oh, and what about the report on the shotguns you were looking into?"

"Oh that. I haven't turned up anything of interest," Mulholland said.

"Hmm, OK. All the best for now."

* * *

"Hi, Maureen, it's Sinéad."

"Oh, hi Sinéad. What's the story?" Lyons said.

"Well, it's a bit of an odd one. The place has been rightly turned over, just like Séan said. But there's definitely no sign of forced entry anywhere, and I've had a proper look around."

"Was the place properly locked up after you had finished there the day of the murder?"

"It certainly was. I saw to it myself before I left."

"Hmm. So maybe it was someone who had a key then. I wonder who had keys to Ann Sweeney's house?" Lyons said.

"Search me."

"And I suppose there are no new conveniently placed fingerprints either?"

"Afraid not. In fact, there are very few sets of prints here at all except for the woman and of course her son."

"OK. How are you getting on collecting up the books?"

"Just finishing up now. I roped in two of Séan's lads and my jeep is now jammed with ten cardboard boxes full of the things. There's hardly room for me in it."

"Have you got them all – the books, I mean?"

"Yep! Every last one. The place looks really weird without them. Kind of naked or something," Loughran said.

"OK. Well, get them back here to me as soon as you can. I have an appointment at the University tomorrow and I'd like to take one or two over with me."

* * *

The books were delivered to Mill Street mid-afternoon, and Lyons recruited a couple of uniformed Gardaí to help John O'Connor go through them all and cross reference them to the spreadsheet on Ann Sweeney's computer. By eight o'clock the daunting task had been completed, and

O'Connor came into Lyons' office clutching a few sheets of paper.

"Right boss, we're done," O'Connor said.

Lyons took the sheets of paper that the young man was offering and glanced at them.

"Just give me the heads-up, John. I'm too tired to wade through any more spreadsheets."

"OK. Well, we cross-referenced all the books that Sinéad brought in against the computer. There are four books missing, all of them are coloured green on the spreadsheet and have a value of several thousand euro, according to the valuations on the computer. I haven't had a chance to research the value on the web, but I can do that tomorrow morning."

"Interesting. Thanks, John, and thank the lads for all their good work too, that wasn't easy. Oh, and could you leave me a couple of the other books highlighted in green too. I'm going over to the University tomorrow and I'd like to take them with me to show to the librarian."

"Sure, no problem. Anything in particular you'd like?"

"No. I'm not going to read them, I'll just show them to what's-her-name, see what she thinks."

Lyons' phone rang.

"Hi, it's me," Mick Hays said as soon as she answered. "I'm sitting here in An Béal Bocht, and your wine is getting warm!"

"God, you're a lifesaver, Mick. I'll be there in five minutes."

An Béal Bocht, which translated from Irish means 'The Poor Mouth', was a trendy bistro not too far from the station that Hays and Lyons liked to frequent. At the front of the premises there was a busy bar where three bartenders just about kept up with the constant demand for drinks. To the rear of the place, tables were arranged for diners, and it was a good deal quieter. Hays sat facing the door, and it was barely a few minutes before his partner appeared, looking remarkably good, he thought, after a tough day of detecting.

He got up and gave Lyons a kiss on the cheek.

"Hi! You look great. This murder mystery stuff obviously agrees with you," Hays said as they took their seats.

"Don't, will ye," Lyons said, taking a decent swig of her glass of chardonnay which was still just about the right temperature.

Their waiter arrived at the table, full of cheer.

"Evening, folks. I see you have the menus, but I have heard that the chef has some very nice roast lamb that he's keeping as a secret. I guess he's hoping no one will order it and then we'll get to have it later," the man said with a broad smile.

"Well, now, I guess we might just have to spoil that for him. What do you say, Maureen?"

"Sounds great, and tell him not to stint on the portions, I'm starving!"

"Excellent. Are you OK for drinks?"

"You say all the right things, Aidan. Thanks – I could do with a top-up," Lyons said, and Hays nodded confirming that he too would like some more wine.

The waiter collected up their menus and went off to busy himself with their order.

"So, what's the story?" Hays said.

"There isn't one, Mick. This is a right old puzzle. I suppose you heard that the woman's house was broken into and some of her precious books stolen. Right under Séan Mulholland's nose too. Sometimes I think he's a bit past it."

"Ah, now don't go blaming Séan. He's not used to grisly killings on his patch – not human ones anyway. He's a good cop, and a decent man as well, but I can see you're a bit frustrated by it all," Hays said.

"You know me too well! Yes, I am. Any ideas?"

Just then, Aidan came back balancing two plates loaded with roast lamb, carrots, broccoli, and roast potatoes, and holding a bottle of wine by the neck between two fingers.

"Thanks, Aidan. Looks delicious. Sorry to eat your dinner," Hays said.

"Don't worry, there's plenty more for us later." He winked at Lyons as he filled both their glasses with a decent measure of chilled white wine.

"Ideas. Let's see. Have you got hold of her bank accounts yet?"

"No. We've been too busy running around trying to sort out the murder and the break-in," Lyons said.

"Well, you know what I always say, foll–"

"Yes, I know, 'follow the money'. The old reliable Mick Hays method of detection," Lyons said, interrupting him.

"Don't scoff. You know it usually works, or at least it's worked for me over the years."

"Yes, I'm sorry. I don't mean to be churlish, it's just this thing has me driven mad. You're right, of course. I'll get John onto it first thing. Thanks," she said, holding up her glass and clinking it against his.

Chapter Eleven

As soon as John O'Connor arrived into work the next morning, Lyons called him into her office.

"Morning, John. Listen, today I want you to concentrate on Ann Sweeney's money trail. You know the drill – bank accounts, savings, credit cards – all the usual. I want to see if she had any real money anywhere, and if she did, where it was coming from. And if you do find anything interesting, get Eamon to help with the banks, or whatever. You know they'll pull the old GDPR trick to stay shtum, but Eamon knows how to deal with that nonsense."

"Right, boss. Anything else?"

"No, that's it. But let me know when the coffee run is on. I need something to kick start me this morning!" Lyons said.

"No problem. I'll nip across now if you like."

"Great thanks. Hang on. Here's some money. Get some doughnuts as well and coffee for whoever is out there. Mine's a cappuccino," Lyons said handing O'Connor a nice crisp €50 note.

* * *

By lunchtime, Lyons was ready for a break from the office. She was glad that she had the appointment at the University to punctuate the afternoon. She grabbed two of the books that had been highlighted in green on Ann Sweeney's spreadsheet, and set off.

Lyons had expected Miranda Tregaron to be a rather frumpish middle-aged woman with short cropped hair and a wrinkled face, dressed in a print frock and flat shoes. How wrong she was.

When the woman came out to meet Lyons after she was announced at the library, Lyons had to do a quick reset. Tregaron was just about six feet tall with long, dark blonde hair and a stunning figure. She was dressed in designer denim jeans and a navy polo shirt, and her high cheekbones and ice blue eyes, together with the fact that she was probably no more than thirty-four or five years old, definitely left an impression.

"Good afternoon, Inspector. I'm Miranda Tregaron," she said in a pronounced south-west of England accent, extending her hand towards Lyons.

"Hello. Thank you for seeing me, Ms Tregaron, I'm sure you're very busy."

"It's no problem, and it's Miranda, by the way. We don't stand on ceremony here. Shall we go to my office?"

Tregaron turned and led the way along the book-lined corridors to a small office at the back of the library. The office was immaculately set out, with a small but tidy desk upon which was perched an Apple MacBook. There was a pile of books alongside the computer, and a telephone at the other side. A number of waist-high bookcases lined the three walls around the room, all arranged in size order. A visitor's chair was positioned in front of the desk, and Lyons sat in it.

"Can I get you a coffee, or tea, Inspector?" Tregaron enquired.

"No, I'm fine thanks, but have one yourself if you like."

"It's OK. I drink too much of the stuff anyway."

"If you don't mind me saying so, I think I detect a British accent. May I ask where you are from?"

"Cornwall. I studied English Literature at Bristol University and then made the mistake of falling for the charms of an Irishman, which is how I ended up here. But it's good. I love my job, and the team here is terrific. We all get along famously."

"Ah, OK." Lyons looked carefully at the woman's hands, but could see no sign of a ring. She decided not to probe further for the moment.

"So, what can I do for you, Inspector?"

Lyons put the two books on the desk and pushed them gently towards the librarian.

"We're investigating a rather brutal slaying that took place out in Clifden recently. You may have seen it reported in the paper or on the news."

"Yes, I heard about it on Galway Bay FM. Shocking – the poor woman. But what have these got to do with it?" Tregaron said, nodding towards the two volumes.

"The victim was big into books. She appears to have quite a collection, and some of them are first editions and may be quite valuable," Lyons said.

"And these are two of them, I presume. May I?"

"Yes, of course."

Tregaron donned white cotton gloves, picked up the topmost book and opened it carefully. It was a volume of some two hundred and fifty pages, and the edges were stained brown from ageing. The cover had gold lettering on the spine, and inside, the book claimed to have been printed more than a hundred years ago. She skimmed through the opening pages, and then examined it from outside more particularly.

"Well, it looks exactly as you say. A first edition. And you are right, it should indeed be quite valuable. But in these cases, we like to authenticate the books very carefully. Do you think I could hold onto this one for a few days and have it looked at?"

"Yes, sure. I was hoping you might be able to do that for us. But I'll need to get a receipt. It's just a formality, you understand, but these may turn out to be evidence," Lyons said.

"Of course. That's not a problem. We have a form for that. It's not unusual for us to get books to appraise for one of the collections," Tregaron said reaching into the top drawer of her desk and taking out an official-looking pad.

"Are there many more like this?" Tregaron said.

"Yes, quite a number. I have a list that I can let you have if you like?"

"Let's see what this one tells us first."

"How long will it take you to examine it?"

"I'll give it to Gerard as soon as we're finished here and he should have some word tomorrow. He loves this sort of thing."

"Great. Can I leave the other one with you too?"

"OK. No problem. It's not often books get involved in serious crime. The literary set are a bit more law-abiding than that, usually."

"Right, well I'll leave these with you then, Miranda. Oh, and will there be any charge?" Lyons said.

Tregaron smiled.

"Not at all. We provide a service to the book trade especially for rare copies. We are fully state-funded."

"Great. Thanks so much, Miranda," Lyons said giving the librarian a business card, "maybe you'd give me a call when you have something?"

"Yes, of course. Nice to meet you. I'll see you out."

On the way back out of the complex, Lyons learned that Tregaron's love interest in her Irishman hadn't lasted very long, and she was now single and lived on campus in a grace-and-favour apartment that went with the job.

Travelling back to the station, Lyons revisited the meeting in her head.

"Well, just goes to show how wrong you can be. I'm not letting Mick anywhere near her, that's for sure!"

Chapter Twelve

John O'Connor knocked on Lyons' door.

"Come in, John. Take a seat," she said.

"Thanks, boss. You asked me to look into Ann Sweeney's finances," O'Connor said, offering a few A4 pages to Lyons across the desk. "It's quite interesting. She has an account with the local bank in Clifden. Nothing strange there. The usual utility bills, ATM withdrawals, her pay from the library going in every month, a bit of extra from Social Welfare and a monthly payment of €500 that I traced back to her ex-husband."

"Right. Is there much in the account?"

"No. Only around €220 at the moment, but she's due her pay any day so that will top that up."

"How much does she get paid from the library?"

"Not a lot. It varies a bit. I presume that reflects some extra days working now and then, but it's usually around €600. That's net of course. It would be a bit more before tax is deducted. But there's more," O'Connor said.

"Go on."

"I found an app on her laptop for a bank in the Netherlands. The icon wasn't on the desktop, so I think she had meant to hide it, or at least make it a bit less obvious. It's for Rabobank, and from what I can see, the account is held in Utrecht."

"I see. Have you been able to get the balance?"

"No, not yet. The bank has some pretty tight security on the account. I've tried a few things, but I can't get into it – not yet anyway. I may have to go the official route, which could take weeks to sort out."

"Right, well keep at it. Even the fact that she had an overseas account is interesting. Let me know if you find anything. And could you ask Sally to come in for me?"

"Sure, no problem."

A few minutes later, Sally Fahy appeared at the door.

"Hi, boss. What's up?" Fahy said.

"Come in, Sally. Grab a seat. Tell me, have you met Ann Sweeney's son, Dónal, yet?"

"No. It was Eamon that went to break the news to him. Why?"

"OK, well I think you should pay him a visit. He lives in a student place up on Moyola Park, number 23 if memory serves. I want to find out if he knew anything about what his mother was up to with all those books. And if he knew she had an offshore bank account."

"Oh, OK. But why me?"

"Why do you think? You're a good-looking girl and he's a twenty-year-old bloke. Just let a bit of chemistry work its magic, get him to open up to you a bit. You never know what you might find out," Lyons said.

"You mean you want me to exploit the fact that he's just lost his mother and flirt shamelessly with him?"

"That's about it, yeah. You up for it?"

"Course! But best keep our tactics just between ourselves, don't you think, boss?"

"Definitely. If you call on him before midday, he'll probably be in his PJs or maybe even his boxers."

Fahy laughed as she got up to leave the room, shaking her head.

* * *

"Lyons," she said, as she picked up the phone. It was late in the afternoon, and Lyons was looking forward to getting home. It had been a trying day.

"Ah, Inspector, I'm glad I've caught you. It's Gerard Mayhew here from UCG. Miranda gave me one of your books to have a look at earlier."

"Ah, yes, she said you'd give it the once over. Have you found out anything?"

"I'd prefer not to talk about it over the phone. Do you think you could stop by tomorrow morning, maybe, say around ten?"

"Yes, of course. Where will I find you?"

"They hide me away at the very back of the library block in a kind of Portakabin thing. Just follow the track around the main library and you'll see it near where they have the boiler house and the waste collection area. There's a glass door in the middle of the building. You can just come straight in."

"OK, thanks, Mr Mayhew, I'll see you tomorrow at ten."

* * *

Lyons arrived home at more or less the same time as Mick Hays. She changed out of her work clothes, and set about preparing a meal for the two of them. They ate in silence until their plates were clean.

"Compliments to the chef," Hays said, as he wiped his mouth with a paper napkin, "that was scrumptious. Thanks. Coffee?"

"Yes, please."

"I'll just clear away and then see to it. You go and sit down, love."

When the coffee was made, Hays brought it through to the lounge and set it down on the low table in front of the settee.

"So, how's the Sweeney thing going?" he said.

"Slowly. But we may be getting somewhere. Looks like she may have been up to something with the books, but I don't know what yet. I'm sending Sally out to talk to the son again. See if he knows what's been going on."

"Good plan."

"Oh, and if there is something going on with the books, I may have to make it up with Inspector Wallace. Not looking forward to that."

"Ah, don't worry, he'll be fine. If you like I can soften him up a bit for you."

"Nah, it's OK. He might even be glad to get the call. We'll see. Oh, by the way, I had a call from Sheila earlier. Séamus has to go into hospital for some tests. He's been off his food lately and doesn't feel too good."

"Oh, sorry to hear that. Does she want you to go over?" Hays asked.

"Not at the moment, but I might pop over at the weekend just to give her some sisterly support. You can come if you like."

"We'll see. I wouldn't mind going out for a walk across the fields with Séamus. I like him, and you never know, he might open up a bit more to another bloke about whatever ails him. You know what us guys are like when it comes to anything medical."

"Yes, I do, which is why I'm glad that you have to have an annual check-up for the job. Gives me great peace of mind."

"Ah, don't worry, there's a good bit of life left in the old dog yet. I'll demonstrate later if you like!"

"Ah, you're OK, I believe you. Anyway, I'm all in. This Sweeney thing is frustrating the hell out of me."

Chapter Thirteen

It was a dull and dreary west of Ireland day the following morning when Lyons got up and made breakfast for the two of them. Heavy grey clouds were blowing in from the Atlantic Ocean where they had picked up literally tons of water from the sea as they crossed from the east coast of the United States. Salthill, where Lyons lived with Hays, was the first landfall that the clouds encountered, so they wasted no time in shedding their load in the form of heavy persistent rain. By the look of it, it was down for the day.

Lyons decided to go straight to the University to keep her date with Gerard Mayhew. She parked her Volvo as close to the Portakabin that Mayhew had described as she could, and dashed inside through the glass door, which, as Mayhew had said, was unlocked. Once inside, she shook the surplus rainwater off her jacket, and used the window glass for reflection as she did her best to straighten out her hair which had been mussed up by the strong, wet breeze.

There was no reception area, so she walked down the corridor and soon spotted a man in his fifties seated behind a chaotic desk inside a small room off the passage way. She knocked and opened the door.

"Mr Mayhew?" she said.

"Yes. Oh my gosh, is it that time already," the man said getting up from a very worn but sturdy leather-faced chair, "you must be Inspector Lyons."

"Yes, Maureen Lyons," she said extending her hand and shaking his.

Mayhew was about five foot nine in stature; overweight, with a modest amount of thin grey hair arranged in a comb-over across his otherwise bald head. He wore a tweed jacket and an open-necked green shirt that may well have fitted him when he was two sizes smaller, but now struggled to contain his middle-aged spread.

"Come in, come in. Take a seat, Inspector. Nice to meet you."

The two sat down, and Mayhew shuffled a pile of books that were perched precariously on the edge of the desk.

"Well, well, you have brought me in an odd one, Inspector," he said, opening the book that Lyons recognised from the collection that had been retrieved from Ann Sweeney's house. It was titled *When We Were Very Young* by A. A. Milne.

"How's that, Mr Mayhew?"

"On the face of it, this looks just like an original first edition. It's aged appropriately, and has all the correct markings on the detail page at the front. It should be worth about €7,000, but all is not what it seems."

"Oh, go on."

"Well, as you can see, the first page of the book has been glued to the front cardboard cover. That's standard procedure. It gives strength to the structure of the volume and helps to prevent it falling apart. But when this book first came out, the glue that they used would have been animal glue, probably made from horses' hooves or something. But the glue in this book is a modern PVA substance. Definitely not around in the 1920s. And there's more."

"I see," Lyons said, trying to get the image of melted horse hooves out of her mind.

"Yes, the paper isn't right. When this book was originally printed, the paper would have been made of wood pulp. In about 1990, that became unpopular with the tree huggers and eco-warriors, so the industry switched to using recycled cardboard and even rag waste for papermaking. I've looked at this under a microscope, and there's no sign of wood fibres in the paper at all. This is new stuff."

"I see. So, this is a forgery then?"

"There's one final test that we did which is conclusive. In the 1920s books were printed using wet ink. The ink soaked into the paper a little and was therefore permanent. This book was printed on a laser printer – probably a big industrial job that provides a lot of control over the fonts, spacing and so on," Mayhew said.

"How can you tell?"

"A trade secret, Inspector, but I'll share it with you. We removed two pages from the middle of the book and cooked them in a microwave oven. When they had been in there for a few minutes, we removed them and used a paintbrush to brush away all the ink from the pages, leaving them more or less blank," Mayhew said retrieving two brown blank pages from a drawer and showing them to Lyons.

"Cripes! How does that work?"

"Laser printers use a magnetised plastic ink in powder form. It's called toner. The paper is charged with an electrical charge by the printer where the words go, and toner is sprinkled across it. The ink sticks to the magnetised parts, and then the paper is put through heated rollers that melt the ink and fix it to the page. But a microwave oven re-melts the ink, and you can just brush it away. That's why inkjet printing is used for most official government documents such as work permits, because inkjet ink acts like the old stuff and seeps into the fabric of the page," Mayhew said sitting back in his chair.

"Good Lord! That's amazing. I didn't know any of that. So how old is the book then?"

"Hard to be precise, but I'd say no more than a year or two, if that."

"But it looks so old. It's all brown at the edges of the pages, and there are some brown spots on the fly leaf," Lyons said, handling the book again.

"That's all pretty easy to do, Inspector. Forgers often use cold tea applied with a paintbrush to the edges of the book when it's closed. And those spots you mention are called foxing. Again, easy to mimic. They often use women's makeup for those."

"I see. But surely a collector would spot those inconsistencies a mile off?"

"Ah, well now, that's where the cleverness comes in. You are quite correct. A reputable dealer or an auction house would spot it at once, but these people sell these to private collectors. They are often captains of industry, or wealthy bankers or something. For them, it's owning the thing that is important. They never read the books, they just put them into a bookshelf in their dining room and impress their visitors with them. And the sellers usually build up a trust relationship with their targets too by selling them a couple of genuine first editions initially in case they have them checked out. Once trust is established, they can slip in a few of these easily enough, and if it comes to light, the seller can claim to have been duped as well."

"Seems like a lot of fuss just to flog a few dodgy books. What kind of money do these things make?" Lyons said.

"Oh, it's well worth it, don't worry. Some of these sell for tens of thousands of euro. Even the more common ones can fetch five or ten thousand, and you know, it's odd, the bigger the price, the easier they are to dispose of. The kind of people that buy them believe that the more they pay, the better the deal."

"And have you any insight into who these people are, Mr Mayhew?"

"You mean the crooked dealers? No, not at all. That's your job, Inspector. We occasionally authenticate rare books for private collections and libraries, but I've never had reason to dig into where these things are coming from."

Lyons thanked the man profusely for the information he had provided. She collected the two books, and set off back to the station. She had a lot to think about. The rain had become even heavier when she got back outside, and on the short hop to her car, she got a good dousing. Once inside, she had to use the fan on full blast to clear the steam from the inside of the glass, and once she could see, she made her way slowly back to the Garda station at Mill Street.

Chapter Fourteen

Sally Fahy was having her own struggle with the weather.

"How come the traffic is always ten times worse when it rains?" she said to herself, inching along the slick city streets on her way to see Dónal Sweeney. When she arrived at Moyola Park, there was no on-street parking to be found, and she was determined she wasn't going to park too far away, given the teeming rain. She decided to leave the car across the driveway of number 23, blocking in the little silver Toyota. She put the 'Garda on duty' notice in the windscreen, hoping that she wouldn't cause to much inconvenience for whoever owned the car.

Fahy dashed to the front door, and stood in as close as she could to the building to try and avoid the deluge that was coming down from the blocked gutters overhead. She rapped firmly on the glass-panelled door. She could hear loud music coming from inside the property, but no one came to the door. She was getting soaked. She thumped heavily on the door again, losing patience, and a moment later she could see a dark shape approaching through the frosted glass of the front door. A tall, thin young man dressed in a T-shirt and shorts answered.

"Yes, what do you want?" he said in a rather surly manner.

"I'm here to see Dónal. Can I come in please, I'm getting soaked?"

The lad said nothing, but stood aside allowing Fahy to enter the rather squalid premises. The young man eyed her up and down a few times, and muttered something about Dónal's luck changing.

"Do you think you could get him for me?" Fahy said.

"Upstairs. First on the right. But he's not up yet, so he could be naked," the man said with a leer, admiring Sally's backside as she ascended the stairs.

Fahy knocked on Dónal's door and announced herself. She heard a muffled response from inside the room which she interpreted as an instruction for her to wait a minute. Then, she heard "Come in" from the other side of the door and she went in.

The room was in a terrible state. There were clothes everywhere, particularly on the floor. Three empty and quite dirty pint glasses stood on the nightstand along with a CD player and an indescribable handkerchief. The duvet was scruffy too, and the one window in the room looked as if it hadn't been cleaned in several years.

"Hi, Dónal," she said, introducing herself. "I was hoping we could have a wee chat," Fahy said looking around the room. She would have liked to sit down but couldn't see anywhere that looked safe, so she remained standing.

"Oh, OK. What do you want to know?"

"Look. Have you had breakfast yet?" Fahy said.

"No, of course not. Why?"

"Well, let's get out of here and go somewhere and I'll treat you. How does that sound?"

"Yeah, OK. Give me five minutes to get dressed, and I'll see you downstairs," Sweeney said.

Fahy wondered if this was a ruse to allow the boy to escape somehow. But she felt the lure of a decent meal would probably overcome any tendency for him to take flight.

She stood in the hallway while Dónal had a quick wash and put on some proper clothes. He came crashing down the stairs a few minutes later and shouted to the only other occupant of the house, "See you later, Todd. OK, let's go!"

Fahy drove back towards the city and found a parking place almost directly outside a small modern cafe, painted in fashionable pale grey and boasting 'All day breakfast' in the window for a modest €6.99.

"This OK?" Fahy said to her passenger.

"Yeah, great, thanks."

Inside, Sweeney ordered the Full Irish, while Fahy settled for a large coffee and a muffin. When Sweeney had devoured almost half of the large plateful of food that had been put before him, he said, "Well, what's on your mind, Sergeant?"

"Ah, nothing specific. I just wanted to have a chat about you and the family. This must have been a dreadful shock for you. How are you coping?"

"OK, I guess. Dad is quite supportive, even though I don't live with him. But he calls me every day, and I've been out to his place a couple of times. I think he's really sorry that they didn't make a go of it."

"So, what went wrong?"

"Hard to say, really. He was always very busy, and took Mum for granted. He left her to do all the house stuff and was often either working late or away somewhere. She just got fed up with it. It wasn't her idea of a marriage."

"Was there someone else in her life?"

"No, I don't think so at any rate. I never copped it if there was. Don't get me wrong, Mum was a good-looking woman. She could have had her choice of men, but after Dad I think she was put off the whole idea."

Fahy tried to reconcile this information with what Bridget O'Toole had told the Gardaí about frequent late-night male visitors to Ann Sweeney's house in Clifden.

"Did you see your dad much after they split up?"

"Quite a bit, actually. He used to come out to Clifden sometimes at the weekend and we'd go shooting rabbits out on the headland near Dog's Bay. There's millions of them out there."

"So, your dad has a shotgun then?"

"Yep. He has a few in fact. He has a lovely pair of Purdeys. He got them for next to nothing from a house clearance in the UK several years ago. But they are beautiful guns. So easy to use and very little recoil if you hold them properly tight against your shoulder. And he has another 12-bore too, more of a utilitarian one," Dónal said.

"Are they all 12-bores?"

"No, they're not. The Purdeys are a kind of his and hers set. Quite unusual, I think. They don't make them anymore. The man's gun is a 12-bore, but the woman's is 20-bore. That's a bit lighter and less powerful, but it did me fine. The rabbits are easy targets at certain times of the day."

"I see. Sounds like fun," she said, thinking quite the opposite. Why anyone should call slaying harmless fluffy-tails fun was beyond her.

By this time Dónal had polished off all of his breakfast, and Fahy was anxious to get back to the station and share this new-found information with the rest of the team. When she had paid the bill for them both, they put on their jackets and went outside.

"Thank God the weather's improved a bit. Can I drop you back at the house?" Fahy said.

"No, it's OK thanks, Sergeant. I think I'll walk, blow away the cobwebs. But thanks. I enjoyed that. I don't suppose you'd like to come out for a drink with me some evening after work?" he said, looking into her pale blue eyes.

"Hmm, can I get back to you on that one, Dónal? But thanks for asking," she said smiling warmly.

* * *

When Fahy got back to the station, she brought Lyons up to date with the new information.

"Excellent, Sally! I knew it was a good idea to send you out to see him. Well done," Lyons said.

"Yeah, and he only asked me out too!"

"I'm not surprised. Did you knock him back?"

"Not totally. I said I'd think about it. We might need to get some more from him before this thing is over."

"OK, better still. Now, can you arrange a briefing as soon as possible. This new stuff is very useful and we need to put a few things in motion."

"Righto, I'll try for five o'clock. Is that OK?"

"Yep, perfect. Cheers."

Chapter Fifteen

At just after five o'clock, the detectives were all assembled in the open plan when Lyons came into the room.

"OK, let's get on, everyone. Sally, can you start? Tell us what you found out from Dónal Sweeney."

Sally Fahy told the group about the conversation she had had with the young man in the cafe.

"So, you see, Mr Sweeney Senior is now a person of interest. He has guns that he didn't fess up to, and he has no alibi either. And we know it's often the nearest and dearest that are involved in these cases, so I think we should bring him in for a chat, perhaps under caution. I'll have a word with Mick when we are finished here and see what he says. John, what have you got from tracing Ann Sweeney's cash?"

"I've made some progress, boss. That stupid app that she has for online banking with Rabo reset itself overnight and gave me three more shots at logging in, and I got it on the second attempt. Easy really, it was Dónal's birthday. I don't know why I didn't think of it first."

"Yes, well never mind all that," Lyons said rather impatiently, "what does the account tell us?"

"She has over a hundred grand on deposit with them. It appears to have arrived at various times not regularly spaced, and in unequal amounts, typically five or eight thousand at a time or thereabouts," O'Connor said.

"What period of time are we talking about?" Flynn asked.

"It goes back about three years, boss."

"So, just about the time when she split from the hubby. Interesting," Eamon Flynn said.

"Yes, and there's more. I was out at UCG earlier and spoke to a Mr Mayhew about one of the books that she had in her house. They are forged first editions. No doubt about it," Lyons said.

"Wow! Any idea where they were made, or anything?" Fahy said.

"No, not yet at least. Mayhew isn't finished with them yet. He may be able to get some further information from the paper that was used, but don't hold your breath. This of course means we'll have to get the lovely Inspector Paul Wallace from Dublin involved. But listen, folks, I don't want this to turn into his gig. We've had a vicious killing right here on our patch, and that's the crime we need to solve. Iffy books are obviously part of it, or maybe not, but our focus should be on the killing. Got it?" Lyons said, looking to her team for confirmation that they understood.

"Yes, boss," they said in unison.

"Good. OK, then, jobs for tomorrow. Eamon, can you go out and lift Mr Sweeney and bring him in for a chat. Make sure to get the two Purdeys as well, they need to go to Sinéad for forensic examination. Don't arrest him unless he resists, we don't want him all lawyered up just yet. And by the way, who went to inspect his shotguns?"

"That was Garda Joe Reilly, boss. I'll have a word," Flynn said.

"Yes, please do. John, can you get Sweeney's registration number and scour whatever CCTV you can find for the night in question, see if you can spot it on the move out west."

"Yes, sure, boss. Do you want me to continue the money trail too?"

"Yes, but focus on Sweeney first. See if you can get a ping from his mobile phone anywhere near the scene that fits too, will you? And when you've done that, start looking at Sweeney's finances. If he is up against it, it could provide a motive. Then get stuck into Mrs Sweeney's computer. You know, emails, correspondence, websites visited and all the usual."

"That's a lot to do, boss, do you think I could get some help?"

Lyons looked across at Sally Fahy, who took the hint.

"OK, John, I'll give you a hand tomorrow unless something urgent comes up."

"Great, thanks, Sarge."

"OK, that's it for now. Let's make an early start in the morning and get on with things. I can feel we're getting a bit nearer to solving this mess now. Off you go," Lyons said.

Lyons retreated to her office and looked up Paul Wallace's number and dialled. It went immediately to voicemail, and Lyons left a message for the man to call her as soon as possible.

"He's probably out on the golf course," she said to no one in particular, but she had barely finished the thought when her mobile started ringing.

"Lyons," she said.

"Good evening, Inspector, it's Paul Wallace. You were looking for me."

"Crikey, that was quick. Were you there all along?"

"No, I'm out on a job, but I have my office phone programmed to call my mobile if I get a message, so here I am. What can I do for you?"

"I think I owe you an apology, Inspector." She went on to explain what had come to light about Ann Sweeney's first editions.

"Hmm, just as we thought. Listen, I think I should travel to Galway tomorrow. Would you have some time to go through things with me? We could swap information and see if our pooled resources can help to crack your case?"

Lyons was impressed by the diplomacy of the man considering she had shunned his earlier approach.

"Yes, I think that could be very useful, thanks. And look, I'm sorry about before, I was out of order."

"No worries, but don't you think first names might be better now that we are on the same side as it were? I'm Paul."

"Yes, of course, I'm Maureen. What time do you think you'll get here tomorrow?" Lyons said.

"I'll be there before you've finished your corn flakes, Maureen, I'm an early riser."

"Oh, OK. See you then."

"Bye."

When Lyons had finished with the call, she went looking for Mick Hays to bring him up to date. He was in his office.

"Hi, you," he said as she knocked and went in at his invitation.

"Hi. I'm just about finished for the day. How about you?"

"Well, I could leave everything for the night if you wanted to persuade me. Hungry?" Hays said.

"I've just had a large portion of humble pie, but yeah, I guess. Got anything in mind?"

"Wallace?"

"Yeah, how did you know?"

"I'm a detective, remember?"

"Ha ha, very funny. I hope you haven't got my phone bugged."

"Nah, it had to happen. Anyway, what's the story?"

"He's coming down tomorrow early doors. Oh, and we're lifting Ann Sweeney's husband too. He lied about not having several guns, one of which is a 20-bore Purdey," Lyons said.

"Nice. Do you think it was him?" Hays said.

"Possibly, but I don't think so. I know it looks bad for him, but I don't feel it in my bones, as it were. We'll see. I could be wrong."

"Unlikely. But anyway, where to go for eats?"

"O'Conaires?"

"Sounds good. I'll just give them a quick call, and then I'll be with you."

When they were seated in the restaurant, Lyons asked Hays, "So what's going on in your world that I should know about?"

"Quite a bit. The Super is leveraging the good clear-up rate that we have managed to achieve to put some pressure on the suits in the Park for more resources. We're badly in need of some new technology, not to mention some big, better, squad cars. He thinks now that all the new motorways have opened up around here, he can nab a few BMW 4x4s for Roads Policing."

"Cool, I hope he gets one for me too," she said, impishly.

"You never know! But don't you like your Volvo?"

"Yes, I do, I love it. But can you imagine the chaos I could cause in a big fuck-off BMW jeep all brightly coloured and flashing lights?"

"The mind boggles. But, yes, I can imagine, quite easily. Sinéad and yourself could have jeep races out in Ballyconneely, and we could make a book on who's fastest."

"Good idea," Lyons said, giggling at the thought of it, as their food arrived which was every bit as good as expected.

Chapter Sixteen

When Lyons arrived at the Garda station just after half past eight the following morning, Paul Wallace was seated in reception beside a woman in her mid-thirties. He stood up as soon as he saw Lyons.

"Good morning, Maureen. This is Ciara Long, my sergeant. I thought it best to bring her with me too. She's been heavily involved in this case from a while back."

"Hi, Ciara. Sorry I'm a bit late. I hope I haven't kept you waiting?"

"Not at all. We've only just got here," Wallace said.

"Danny here will give you passes, and you can come upstairs with me. I'm not sure if any of the others will be in yet, but we can have a catch-up in any case."

The desk sergeant did the necessary, and all three made their way up to Lyons' office. Lyons sat in behind her desk and removed her jacket, while Wallace and Long took seats facing her.

"OK, well let's go through what we know so far. I think I'll just get Inspector Flynn to sit in too, if that's OK with you?" Lyons said.

"Yes, fine," Wallace said.

Flynn was duly summoned, and brought a chair into the room so that he could sit alongside the two visitors.

"As far as we are concerned, Paul, this is a murder investigation, and a pretty brutal one at that. We know, of course, that there's more to it, but our interest is in solving the murder. Of course, if we can help with your enquiries, all the better," Lyons said.

"And vice versa, Inspector. But I think you may well find that both of these enquiries overlap. We know Ann Sweeney was into forged first editions, and that may very well be why she lost her life. And thanks to you, we now have some hard evidence of her crimes. We hadn't managed to get hold of any of the books until you retrieved them from her house."

"Have you made any specific connection between her death and the forgeries?" Flynn said.

"Not yet, but it's a very sophisticated operation she was involved in. It's more than just a few dodgy first editions," Ciara Long said. "We believe it may be the same gang that are involved in forged currency too."

"Oh. Do tell," Lyons said.

"Recently, we came across a very fancy operation involving the production of forged €50 notes. We think they are being printed in either Poland or the Netherlands. It was very clever. They hide large sheets of them sandwiched between eight foot by four foot MDF. Then they slip a bale containing the notes in with a legitimate shipment and send it in a container to Dublin. When the container is picked up, the driver stops off at a convenient industrial estate where the bale containing the forged notes is unloaded, and then carries on to the customer with the rest."

"Wow. Slick. But how much do they bring in at a time?" Lyons said.

"We think there's around 250 notes on each sheet, and there are twenty-five sheets of MDF in a bale, so twenty-four sheets of dodgy notes. All in all, some €300,000 in each shipment. And the thing is, the notes are almost better than the official ones. Very high quality, so easy to get value for them," Long said.

"But someone has to chop them up and then start using them, and then the people who are supplying them need to be paid and so on. Have you managed to get a handle on any of that?" Flynn said.

"Yes, we have. I don't want to go into all the details just yet, but we've been working with Europol on it for several months now, and we're getting close to being able to take some action," Wallace said.

"But why do you think there's a connection to Ann Sweeney?" Lyons said.

"Printing. We think the dodgy notes and the dodgy books are being printed in the same place. They're into all sorts. Dodgy packages for high-end perfumes, official documents, and maybe even passports. So, if we can nab them, it will be a terrific coup for us all," Long said.

"But why kill Ann Sweeney, if that's what you think happened?" Flynn said.

"We think she may have been skimming money off the top for herself. She has some quite tasty deposits in a bank in the Netherlands, it's a lot more than the share she would normally receive for her part in handling the books. And this gang are completely ruthless. Anyone who tries to double-cross them won't last long. And there's more," Wallace said.

"We know that they use a few specialist 'agents' to do their dirty work. One of them was recorded entering the country a couple of weeks ago through Cork Airport. A nasty type who sometimes uses the name Pavel Berisha, which is Kosovan," Wallace said.

"I see. But Ann Sweeney was killed using a 20-bore shotgun. Not that easy for a foreigner to get hold of, and certainly not something you could travel with. And her husband just happens to have one that he didn't tell us about as well. We're bringing him in for questioning later this morning," Lyons said.

Wallace smiled.

"That's typical Berisha. He will have done his homework, if it was him, and he will have made it look like the husband. And of course, he'll be long gone by now, probably on the ferry to the UK and then on the Eurostar back to the mainland, and probably using a different identity," Long said.

"I still want to talk to the husband. If we don't follow that up, I'll get my arse kicked all over County Galway, even if you are right about this Berisha character. Anyway, how can we help you guys now?" Lyons said.

"We'd like to have access to Sweeney's computer. There may well be emails and stuff on there that will help us to build a case. And we haven't found out yet exactly where the printing is being done, so if we could work with your forensic folks on the paper and so on that was used for the forged books, it could point us in the right direction," Wallace said.

"Sure, that's no problem. I'll get John O'Connor to clone the hard drive from the laptop, and then you can have it. And, Eamon, can you tee up Mayhew out at the library and Sinéad Loughran to work with Paul and Ciara for me?" Lyons said.

"Yes, of course, boss. Then can I go and get Conan Sweeney in for a chat?"

"Yes, and let's keep this conversation to ourselves for the moment, OK, everyone. Just proceed as we normally would, OK?" Lyons said.

When the meeting had concluded and Lyons was on her own in the office again, Sally Fahy put her head around the door.

"Hi, boss, Séan Mulholland was looking for you. Could you give him a call?"

"Right, Sally. Did he say what it was about?"

"No, he wanted to talk to you himself."

"OK, thanks, Sally, I'll call him right away."

84

Chapter Seventeen

Eamon Flynn took Garda Mary Costelloe with him out as far as Ballinasloe to Conan Sweeney's yard. The Mercedes was parked in front of the office, but there was no sign of anyone around.

Flynn and Costelloe got out of the car and went walkabout. Inside one of the large sheds, Costelloe found a man in a high-vis jacket with his head stuck under the bonnet of a digger, working away on the recalcitrant machine.

"Good morning," Mary called out.

The man rose slowly from his position bent over the engine and looked up.

"Hello, Guard, can I help you?"

"We were looking for Mr Sweeney. Is he about?"

"He's just gone into town in the truck to get some MDF. We have a job on over near Clongowna later, and we need some stuff for it. He'll be back in half an hour or so, if you'd care to wait?" the man said.

"I'll just go and talk to my colleague and see what he wants to do. Are you busy at the moment?" Mary asked.

"We are that. Plenty of jobs on, but nothing too big just at the moment. He's waiting for planning permission to start a house build the far side of the town. That'll keep us going for a year or more. It's a very big job."

Mary was impressed with the amount of information this chap was prepared to divulge, so she pressed on.

"And tell me, eh…?"

"Oh sorry, Martin, Martin O'Boyle. I'll not shake hands with you, Guard, I'm filthy from this bloody thing," he said nodding at the digger.

"Tell me, Martin, does Mr Sweeney's son come around here much?"

"Oh, Dónal, you mean. Yeah, he drops in all right. Himself and the boss go off together sometimes in the afternoons if we're not too busy. He's a nice lad."

"How many men does Mr Sweeney employ then?" Mary said, knowing that she was pushing her luck a little.

"It varies, you know. Depends what work we have on. But I'm here all the time, and then there are four others that are regular. Then he takes on a few Polish lads when things get busy."

"Yes, I hear they are great workers, those Polish blokes."

"Listen, I'm just about to take a break. Would you fancy a cup of tea while you're waiting for Conan? He shouldn't be too long now."

"OK, thanks. I'll just go and find Eamon and see you back at the office."

Mary Costelloe didn't want to reveal that Eamon was an inspector for fear that Martin might clam up in the presence of a more senior officer, so she located Flynn and suggested that they keep his rank to themselves during the tea break.

The three of them were seated at a rudimentary table made from an old door standing on two piles of breeze blocks, drinking tea when an Isuzu flat-bed truck with a Palfinger grab hoist fitted just behind the cab rolled into the yard and came to a halt with a squeal of brakes and a cloud of blue diesel exhaust fumes. The truck was well used, and loaded high with timber and bags of plaster as well as other building materials, all held in place with three bright orange ratcheted straps.

Conan Sweeney alighted from the vehicle and came into the makeshift office.

Eamon Flynn introduced himself and Mary Costelloe, keeping back his rank as he did so.

"We were wondering, Mr Sweeney, if you could spare the time to come into Galway with us for a chat?" Flynn said.

Sweeney flinched a little at the suggestion, so Eamon Flynn continued quickly.

"Nothing heavy, we just need to clear up a few details about your poor wife's death. It won't take long. Oh, and we'd like to collect your shotgun on the way too if you don't mind."

Sweeney thought for a minute before replying.

"OK, I suppose, if it will help. But I'll need to be back here this afternoon. We have a job on over at Clongowna, and I don't want to keep the woman waiting," Sweeney said.

On the way out the door, Sweeney turned to Martin O'Boyle and said, "If I'm not back by three o'clock, Martin, will you take the truck over to Mrs Walsh's place and unload the stuff? Then she'll know we're coming at least."

"Fair enough. See you later."

* * *

"You'll have to direct us to your home, Mr Sweeney," Flynn said over his shoulder to the man seated in the back seat of his car alongside Mary Costelloe.

"It's out near Tubbergrellan on the R348. Head out that way, and I'll tell you where to go."

Flynn drove out along the R348, which was a narrow country road with very little housing along its length. When they were some five kilometres out from the town of Ballinasloe, approaching Knocknagréine crossroads, Sweeney spoke up.

"Here we are. Just where those white pillars are. Turn in there. That's my place."

Flynn indicated, slowed and swung the car in between two white-painted pillars that were attached to tall, arched, wrought iron gates that stood open. The house was up a long narrow drive, flanked on either side with pasture that was fenced off with wooden stud railings. In front of the house itself was a large gravelled turning circle, bordered by a low box hedge neatly trimmed.

Sweeney's house was a large no-nonsense double-fronted affair with a slated roof that overhung the walls by a good measure and had carved soffits giving the property an air of opulence. There were two casement windows to either side of the solid panelled front door which stood under a portico with mock Grecian columns. On the first floor, three similar windows sat symmetrically above the lower ones. To the left of the house was a large sun room with a glass roof in the style of an orangery, as opposed to just a conservatory. The impression given was that of some wealth, which was underscored by the excellent condition of the place and the carefully tended gardens immediately surrounding the house.

Flynn stopped the car in front of the house and got out. He opened the back door letting Sweeney out, and then went round to the other side to release his colleague, the doors being set to 'kiddie proof' which was standard procedure when escorting a possible suspect.

"Nice place you have here, Mr Sweeney," Flynn said as they approached the front door.

"It's grand. I built it during the Celtic Tiger years when there was lots of money about, but I don't regret it. It's just a shame that we couldn't all live together here as a family," he said.

Sweeney opened the front door to the sound of an alarm alert going off inside. He went to a keypad located discreetly in the inner porch and tapped in a few numbers, silencing the device.

"I keep the guns in my study," he said, indicating the room at the back of the tiled hall on the left.

"Guns, Mr Sweeney, I thought you said you told us you had only one shotgun," Flynn said.

"I never did. You must have misheard me."

Flynn shrugged.

The three of them went to the room and Sweeney took out a bunch of keys to open a gun safe that was standing partly hidden by the luxurious drapes adjacent to the window looking out to the side of the house over the immaculate lawns. When the gun safe was opened, Flynn could see one double-barrelled shotgun standing upright inside, with its trigger pointing outwards. The cabinet was lined in dark green felt to protect the weapon from any possible scratches as it was taken out or replaced.

"That's odd," he said, "I thought they were both here. Maybe Dónal has the small one. He sometimes borrows it, though he nearly always asks, and he hasn't this time."

"Does he have keys to the house and the gun cabinet, Mr Sweeney?"

"Yes, of course. Why wouldn't he?"

Flynn gestured to Mary Costelloe who took the hint and left discreetly to go outside and call Galway to tell them that Dónal Sweeney may be in possession of a 20-bore shotgun.

"Very well. You may as well leave that one there, Mr Sweeney. It's the 20-bore we're interested in. When did you last see it?" Flynn asked.

"Oh, it must be about two weeks ago. Yes, that's right. It was the last time Dónal and I went rabbiting out west. The weekend before last."

"Before your wife was killed then?"

"Yes. But wait a minute – you can't think that Dónal could have had anything to do with her death? That's preposterous. He loved his mother. He chose her to live with over me, after all," Sweeney said, having some difficulty processing the new information.

"Why don't we just head on into Galway, Mr Sweeney, and you can make a statement and tell us anything you can about this whole business?"

Chapter Eighteen

"Hi, Séan, it's Maureen. You were looking for me."

"Hello, Maureen, yes, thanks for calling back. This could be something and nothing, but I thought you should know anyway," Mulholland said.

"Go on."

"Well, Pascal Brosnan was out at Recess yesterday afternoon. He was just on his rounds, and he noticed a lad doing some work on a camera outside the shop and cafe there. The fella was up a ladder fiddling with the thing, so Pascal engaged him in conversation. It turns out that a delivery van hit the pole where the camera was mounted a few days ago, and deflected the camera so it was looking at the road. The man that runs the shop wanted it put back to focus on the shop doorway. There are steps up to the entrance, and he's afraid he'll get compensation claims if someone trips, or says they have tripped, so he wants the camera for evidence that he's not negligent."

"OK. I get the picture. What else?" Lyons said.

"Well, Pascal had an idea. He asked the shop owner for the recording from the time that the camera was pointing towards the road and took it back to the station in

Roundstone. He reckons it covers the night that Mrs Sweeney was killed."

"Cripes! Nice one, Pascal. Is there anything useful on the film?"

"I'm not sure. Pascal says it's very blurry. It was raining heavily that night and some raindrops got on the lens, but he says there is some activity on it in the wee small hours. He thought your techy folks might be able to do something with it. What do you think?"

"Would there normally be traffic out and about during the night out there, Séan?"

"Ah, not at all, girl. At least not till six in the morning or so. Then you'd get some deliveries going into Clifden, and maybe some people heading into Galway for an early shift or something. But nothing through the night."

"Right, Séan. Can you get Pascal to bring the rest of the footage in here and we'll get working on them to see if we can spot anything of interest?"

"Righto. I'll give him a call and send him in. He'll be there in an hour or so."

"Thanks, Séan."

Sally Fahy was still hanging about when Lyons had finished the call.

"Grab a seat, Sally. I'd like to know what you think about Inspector Wallace's theory."

Fahy sat down and looked straight at her boss.

"Can I be honest, boss?" Fahy said.

"'course," Lyons said.

"I think it's all bullshit. I get that Ann Sweeney may have got entangled with some dodgy books – but Eastern European assassins, nah, I don't think so. What do you make of it?"

"I don't know. Wallace isn't an eejit. And he and his team have spent a lot of time on this whole thing, so there must be something to it. But, like you, I'm sceptical. You know yourself, nine times out of ten these things are down to someone much closer to home. But we'll see. We'd better go along with them for the moment in any case. If it turns out he's right and we have brushed him off, it won't play well upstairs. In the meantime, though, let's see what Eamon gets from the husband. Meanwhile, I want you to stay tight with our two visitors. I don't want them finding out stuff and keeping it to themselves. OK?"

"Yes, sure. They're exploring Ann Sweeney's computer just now. I'll get back out to them."

When Sally Fahy had left the office, Danny, the desk sergeant, called Lyons and asked her to call Mary Costelloe as a matter of urgency. She dialled the number immediately.

"Yes, Mary, what's up?"

"Hello, Inspector. Look, we are out here at Conan Sweeney's house. We came to collect his gun, and it turns out he has two Purdeys, but one of them is missing, and it's the 20-bore. He says his son probably has it."

"Christ! OK, thanks, I'll get someone on it straight away."

When she had finished the call, Lyons summoned Sally Fahy again from the open plan and told her what Mary Costelloe had said.

"You'd better get out to Moyola and lift the lad. Ask him about the gun and if he has it there, bag it and bring it in to Sinéad. Looks like things are breaking in our direction at last."

"OK, boss, I'm on my way."

Fahy took a brightly-coloured squad car and used the blue lights to cut through the afternoon traffic. She pulled up outside the student house in Moyola Park with a squeal of brakes and hopped out. She knocked firmly on the door of the house, and after a few moments it was answered by Dónal Sweeney in person.

"Oh, it's you again. Hi. Come in," Dónal said, standing aside from the door and letting Fahy in. They went through to the kitchen at the back of the house where two other students were sitting around drinking coffee.

"Dónal, I need a word in private," Fahy said.

The other two took the hint, and got up and left the room. When they had gone, Fahy asked the lad, "Dónal, have you got your father's 20-bore Purdey shotgun here in the house?"

"No, of course not. Why would I?"

"Your father says that it's not in his gun cabinet at his house, and he's told us that you probably have it. It seems you are the only other person to have keys to his house and the cabinet. So where is it, Dónal?" Fahy said, looking intently at him.

Dónal took out one of the kitchen chairs and sat down in it, resting his elbows on the table and covering his face with his hands.

"Well?" Fahy said.

"I suppose I may as well tell you," he said dejectedly.

"I think you should."

"It's been nicked, hasn't it?"

"Stolen! When? Have you reported it?" Fahy said, sitting down too.

"No, of course not. And I couldn't tell my father either. He'd go mad. Those guns were the pride of his life."

"When did this happen?" Fahy said.

"A few days ago. I parked the car in the University car park and I think I must have left it open. The gun was in the back seat covered in a blanket, and when I got back to the car, it was just gone. I couldn't believe it. I've been going spare ever since. I thought it might be a prank by one of my mates, but it wasn't. It's gone. What am I going to do? He'll kill me."

"Was this before or after your mother was murdered, Dónal?"

"A while before, but you don't think she could have been killed with that gun, do you?"

"I don't know what to think, Dónal. All I will say is that you're in a right spot of bother now, that's for sure. And not just with your father. You'd better come into town with me. Inspector Lyons will want to talk to you about this. That was pretty dumb leaving it in the car like that, not to mention against the law. Don't you know that shotguns have to be split, with the stock and the barrel transported separately?"

"Yeah, I know. But I was running late for a lecture, so I didn't think."

"Well, get your jacket. You need to come with me."

Dónal stood up and went to get his coat and the two of them left the house and sat into the Garda car.

As Sally Fahy drove back, more sedately this time, towards the Garda station at Mill Street, she asked young Sweeney, "What attempts have you made to recover the gun, Dónal, if any?"

"Well, I keep looking on eBay, Adverts.ie and DoneDeal to see if there's any sign of it, but so far no luck. I put the word out among me mates too, but I can't very well tell everyone in the shooting fraternity, cos it would get back to my dad quick as a wink. Oh, and I put a carefully worded message up on Facebook too, but no response."

Fahy shook her head, and said nothing.

Chapter Nineteen

While Lyons was waiting for both Conan and Dónal Sweeney to arrive separately at the station, she went out into the open plan where she found Paul Wallace and Ciara Long in a huddle with John O'Connor poring over Ann Sweeney's laptop.

"Anything tasty?" she said, as they looked up and acknowledged her presence.

"We're just going through all of her emails. There are some rather odd-looking exchanges between herself and the librarian out in Clifden that might bear some further investigation. And there are emails to someone who calls themselves 'Bastianini', who uses a number of proxy servers to disguise their real location. We haven't come across that name before," Paul Wallace said.

"Who is this Bastianini anyway?" Lyons asked.

"He was a very famous art forger in the nineteenth century. Quite prolific, but of course long since dead," Ciara Long said.

"Terrific. What were they saying to each other?"

"It's all rather tightly coded. Just oblique references to various packages coming and going and so on. We'll have to spend some time trying to decipher what it all means," Wallace said.

"What about McCabe, the library woman? Where does she come in?"

"There are some references to the titles we found in green ink on the spreadsheet. Things like 'arrived today; please collect today'."

"Interesting. Do you think she is involved?" Lyons said.

"Looks a bit like it, but to what extent, we don't know yet," Wallace said.

"OK, well could I ask you guys to pursue that one? We're going to have our hands full with the two Sweeneys for the rest of the day. Maybe you might like to take a trip out to Clifden to talk to the library woman. I'll leave it up to you," Lyons said.

* * *

When Conan Sweeney and his son, Dónal, were placed in separate interview rooms in Mill Street with a uniformed Garda for company, Flynn and Fahy came upstairs to Lyons' office.

"We have the two boyos downstairs now, boss," Flynn said, "how do you want to proceed?"

"I want to interview the young lad with Sally, Eamon. Can you get hold of Mary Costelloe and take a statement from the father? We'll compare notes after and see what's what. Don't let him go till we've had a chat."

"Righto, boss. Let's get on with it then," Flynn said.

* * *

Lyons and Fahy sat opposite Dónal Sweeney in the small interview room on the ground floor of the Garda station.

"Well, Dónal, we need you to tell us all about this gun that you say was stolen. When did you take it from your father's house?" Lyons said.

"I didn't. I had it from the last time we were out shooting rabbits. I just kept it in the car. I wanted to go out again with some of my mates, so I hung onto it."

"And when exactly was that?" Fahy said.

"About two weeks ago."

"So, before your mother was killed, then?" Lyons said.

Dónal just looked at Lyons and his eyes filled with tears.

"When did you last actually handle the gun, Dónal?" Fahy said.

"I dunno. It was on the back seat of the car under a rug. I hadn't touched it for a good few days."

"And was there any ammunition in the car for it?" Fahy said.

"No, I needed to go and get some more. I'd ran out."

"Where do you buy the cartridges?" Lyons asked.

"Dad usually gets them for us. I think there's a place on one of the industrial estates that sells them. The 20-bore ones are a bit unusual. The bloke gets them in specially, I think."

"So, if the person that stole your gun used it to kill your mother, then he or she would have had to buy ammunition. Is that right?" Lyons said.

"I guess. But do you think that was the weapon that was used?" Dónal said, tearing up again.

"We don't know. But there are very few 20-bore shotguns in circulation in these parts, and we know for sure that it was that type of gun."

"God, this is awful. What happens now?" Sweeney said.

"We write up your statement and you sign it. You may face some sort of prosecution over the gun, but that's not up to me. I'll have to have a word upstairs. Then we release you, but don't go too far. We will need to speak to you again."

"OK. What about Dad?"

"We're just taking a statement from him too. We need you to wait till he's finished before we let you go."

* * *

In the next room, Eamon Flynn was questioning Conan Sweeney about the 20-bore shotgun too.

"When did you last see that weapon, Mr Sweeney?"

"It was two weeks ago or thereabouts. Dónal and I had been out near Roundstone shooting rabbits. We bagged a few, and on the way back to Galway we stopped off for a bite to eat in the hotel in Oughterard. Then we drove back to my place where Dónal had left his car, and we put both guns back into the gun cabinet, and locked it, as we always do."

"Are you sure about that, Mr Sweeney? Are you sure Dónal didn't hang onto the gun, or leave it in his car?" Flynn said.

"Yes, I'm certain. I wouldn't have that. We always put the guns back into the safe as soon as we get home. Apart from the fact that they are quite valuable, it's the only practical thing to do. You don't want to leave dangerous weapons lying about."

"No, indeed. What about ammunition for the smaller gun?"

"I keep that in the gun cabinet too. They sometimes go out of stock of the smaller cartridges, so I keep a spare box there all the time."

"And is that definitely the last time you saw the gun?" Costelloe asked.

"Yes, yes, it is."

"Right. Well, we'd like you to stay here for a little longer, Mr Sweeney, till we get this written up and you have signed it. Then you can go," Flynn said getting up to leave the room.

He left Mary Costelloe to sort out the statement, and went looking for Lyons who was back in her office.

"Well?" she said.

"The father reckons that the gun was put back in the gun cabinet at his house the last time himself and the lad went out shooting. What does Dónal say?" Flynn said.

"He says he hung onto it and left it in the back of his car under a blanket, and then it was stolen," Lyons said.

"Well, that's inconsistent, but it could be innocent enough. Certainly not enough to charge either of them with murder, but I'm not happy about it. We'd better let them go. But wait a sec. Didn't Pascal Brosnan have some CCTV that we were supposed to look at?" Lyons said.

"Yes, you're right. Let's go and see if John has been able to make anything of it."

* * *

Lyons and Flynn found John O'Connor at his desk. He was still working on Ann Sweeney's laptop.

"Hi, John. Have you got those CDs that Pascal brought in for us?" Lyons said.

"Yes, they're just here. I haven't had a good look at them though. I've been too busy with the two visitors."

"OK. Well, can we have a look now then?"

"Sure. I'll just load them up on my own PC."

O'Connor placed the first CD into the drive on his desktop and called up the VLC program to play the film.

"Pascal said it was around 3:45 a.m. that something was caught. Wind it on to then will you, John?"

O'Connor pressed a few keys on his keyboard and the image moved along quickly till the time stamp at the bottom of the screen read 3:42. He then slowed it down to normal speed, and the three of them stared at the dull grey image.

"There! Stop it there. Look, there's a vehicle," Lyons said.

O'Connor stopped the playback and rewound for a second or two, and then played it again, this time at half speed.

"God, it's very murky. Can you make anything at all out?" Flynn said.

"Not really, sir. The headlights make the front view all blown out. It's moving quickly too. And the rear view is just a blur," O'Connor said.

"Can we even see what size the vehicle is? Is it a car or a jeep or a van?" Lyons said.

"Hard to tell, boss. I don't think it's a van, but that's all I can say with any certainty. I can copy down the file and send it to the Technical Bureau by email and see if they can get any more from it."

Lyons sighed.

"Yes, OK, John, do that please. And get them to hurry up. We could be looking at the murderer getting away!"

Chapter Twenty

At five o'clock Lyons brought the team together for a briefing.

"Right, let's go round the houses and see what we've got. Can we start with you, Inspector?" she said, looking at Paul Wallace.

"Yes, of course. We've been working on Ann Sweeney's money trail. It's slow-going, but we're beginning to get some kind of pattern now. It seems that she was the one selling many of the forged books from here. We have found her listed on a couple of rare books websites, but there's nothing currently on offer from her."

"Interesting. Have you been to see the woman in the library out in Clifden yet?" Lyons said.

"No, not yet. We're planning on going out there tomorrow morning first thing."

"OK. What about this Pavel Berisha bloke? Any news on him?" Lyons asked.

"He's back in the Netherlands, according to our sources there. He flew out on an Aer Lingus flight from Dublin the day after Mrs Sweeney was found dead in her house," Wallace said.

"Damn. That lends weight to your theory, but why didn't we nab him at the airport?"

"Well, if you recall, Inspector, co-operation had not been established at that time, so we hadn't joined the dots."

"Hmm… OK, no need to rub it in. I've already apologised for that. John, have you anything more from the CCTV in Recess?" Lyons said.

"Not yet, boss. The boys in The Park have only just received it. It will take them a while to work on it and see if they can improve the quality. But I was talking to one of the guys up there, and he says he's not very hopeful. There just isn't enough definition for them to enhance."

"Terrific! Well, you should all know that we have a discrepancy in the statements from Sweeney Senior and Sweeney Junior about the gun, too."

Lyons went on to describe the difference in the two men's statements about the missing 20-bore weapon.

"Is that not enough to bring some charges against the young lad, boss?" Sally Fahy asked.

"Like what, Sally?"

"I don't know. Maybe perverting the course of justice or something. It definitely looks as if there's something fishy going on there."

Paul Wallace cut across Fahy.

"Look, I think it's clear that however he managed it, Pavel Berisha is responsible for the death of Ann Sweeney. He has motive – at least we believe he has. It looks as if Sweeney was holding back considerable sums from the proceeds of the book sales. He had opportunity. After all he was here in the country for several days. And he may well have had the means, if he stole the gun from Dónal Sweeney's car as the boy said."

"Maybe. Is there any way you can get the authorities in the Netherlands to lift him for us?" Lyons said.

"I doubt it. They would need much stronger evidence to issue a European Arrest Warrant, although, unofficially,

I can ask them to keep an eye on him, make sure he doesn't disappear altogether. Now if we had some fingerprint evidence or something tangible to tie him in, then things would be different."

"OK. I'll get back on to Sinéad Loughran and ask her to be absolutely certain that they've gone over the house very thoroughly. I wonder if it might be worth doing a number on Dónal's car too. If Berisha did lift the gun from it, then he may have left a dab somewhere on the car. Have you got a set of his fingerprints for comparison, Paul?" Lyons said.

"I can get them from the Netherlands. They have them on file."

"OK. Well could you do that please. Sally, do you think it's worth having another cosy chat with Dónal on neutral ground?"

"I can try, boss. He was quite open last time we spoke, and we seemed to be getting along OK. Do you want me to try again tomorrow? I can arrange to meet him in a cafe close to the Uni if you like."

"Yes, do that. I've a feeling he has more to tell. And, Eamon, can you go out to Sweeney Senior's yard again. Ask him about the difference in the stories about the gun. And while you're there, have a good snoop around. He may be more a part of this than we realise. OK, everyone, that's it for now. Tomorrow will be busy, so why don't you get off now and we'll chat again in the afternoon, unless anything breaks in the meantime."

Lyons was tidying up her desk, feeling a bit down in the dumps with the lack of progress, when her phone rang.

"Lyons."

"Hello, Maureen, it's Séan here," Mulholland said.

"Oh, hi Séan. How's things?"

"Ah, not so bad, thanks. Listen, I wanted to have a word with you. I was out and about earlier on and I got talking to Bridget O'Toole, you know, the woman from the post office."

"Oh, yes, I remember. Did she have anything interesting to say?"

"She did. She told me that about two days before Ann Sweeney was killed, a man came into the post office with a parcel. He was looking for Ann Sweeney's house. Bridget thought he was a courier, you know, one of those delivery services that everyone uses these days. Bridget pointed him in the direction of the Sweeney house, and thought no more about it."

"Was there anything odd about the delivery driver, Séan?"

"Bridget said he was foreign. She couldn't place the accent, but she said he definitely wasn't Irish or English."

"I see. Do you think it would be worth my while popping out in the morning to speak to her, Séan? I might have some idea of the identity of that man, and I might even be able to bring a photograph," Lyons said.

"Aye, that's a good idea, or if you like you could just send me the photo and I could check it with her. But if you fancy the trip out, that might be better."

"Leave it with me, Séan. I'll give you a call in the morning and let you know what's happening. Thanks for the tip-off."

"Right, so. We'll talk tomorrow."

Lyons dashed outside to try and catch Paul Wallace before he left the station, and found him at the top of the stairs.

"Paul, hang on a minute. Do you have a picture of this Pavel Berisha at all?"

"Yes, I have one in my file. Do you want it?"

Lyons explained the call she had taken from Séan Mulholland, and that she planned to go out to Clifden in the morning to talk to the postmistress.

"Good idea. We may be getting somewhere at last!"

Lyon's phone was ringing when she got back to her office. It was Superintendent Mick Hays.

"Hi. Listen, I just wanted a quick word. The boss has asked me to take Wallace and his sergeant to dinner. Extend the hand of friendship, as it were. Do you fancy it?"

"Yes, of course. I've just seen them leave the station. I presume they've gone back to the hotel."

"OK. Well, I'll call him on his mobile and arrange for us to collect the pair of them at seven-thirty."

"Great. It will give me time to put on my glad rags. Where do you want to take them?"

"Well, it's on expenses, so I was thinking maybe The Meyrick, or The Twelve. What do you think?"

"Let's do The Meyrick. It's handier for their hotel. Oh, and by the way, you're the designated driver. I need alcohol!"

"Fair enough. See you at home in a bit then."

"Yeah, bye."

Chapter Twenty-one

Hays parked his car outside the Imperial Hotel where the two visiting Gardaí were staying and went inside to collect them. It was a fine evening. Not exactly balmy, but certainly not cold, and there was a clear sky and very little wind. Lyons waited in the car till the three others appeared at the door, and then got out, making sure the 'Garda on duty' notice was displayed prominently in the windscreen of Hays' car.

Wallace was dressed much as earlier in a jacket and casual pants, but he had put on a shirt and tie for the occasion. Ciara Long was a different matter. She was sporting an off-the-shoulder black dress and high-heeled shoes, and her hair, which had been tied back in a ponytail earlier, was now styled and hung in gentle waves to her shoulders.

"We may as well walk to the restaurant. It's just across the square," Hays said, nodding at the formidable building which had once been The Great Southern Hotel attached to Galway's main railway station.

Hays fell in with Wallace, leaving Lyons to accompany Ciara Long as they strolled along the side of Eyre Square.

"How long have you been in the Gardaí, Inspector?" Long said by way of conversation.

"Seems like forever, Ciara, and by the way it's Maureen and Mick when we're out. It was here that my career kinda got started." Lyons went on to relate the story of how she nabbed an armed bank robber single-handedly coming out of the TSB when she was a rookie in uniform many years ago.

"Wow! That's amazing. Who would have thought that there was so much crime going on out here in the west of Ireland?" Long said.

"You wouldn't believe the half of it, Ciara. What about you? How long have you been in, and why the Fraud Squad?"

"Like you, I started off in uniform. But then a vacancy came up in Harcourt Street and my sergeant at the time more or less pushed me into it. I think he wanted to get rid of me to be honest. We didn't get on. So here I am. I enjoy the work, and Paul is great. I've learnt a huge amount from him."

Lyons was curious to probe their relationship a bit further, but thought that the men were probably within earshot, so she let it be, for now at least.

* * *

The meal at The Meyrick was truly excellent, as usual. They were seated at a table near the window in the top floor restaurant, and the head waiter made a fuss of them, as Hays was well known to him, and he recognised the dynamic of the foursome. The sommelier produced a couple of bottles of excellent wine which slipped down easily with the food.

As the evening wore on, the group exchanged war stories about the various encounters that they had with lawlessness. Lyons told of the time that she was kidnapped by a thug whom she managed to overpower near the border with the North of Ireland, and the time when she spent the night in a bog hole after a vengeful villain had tried to do away with her.

"Crikey! You've had quite a few adventures, Maureen. And here's us thinking all you guys had to deal with was a few stray donkeys and a bit of after-hours drinking. Just shows how wrong you can be," Wallace said.

"Tell me about it. And this current caper looks as if it might be quite big too. Do you get many of these to deal with?"

"A lot of our time is spent these days on cybercrime of one kind or another. The criminal classes have discovered that it's a lot safer to sit at home in front of a screen than tooling up and running into a bank or post office shouting the odds. More profitable too. Ciara here has a real talent with this stuff. I just step up at the last minute and take all the credit, isn't that right?" Wallace said smiling at his colleague.

"That's about it. No, but seriously, you wouldn't believe the scams that we encounter. And people are so gullible. It's moved on a lot since the letters from Nigerian banks telling you that there was several million dollars awaiting you if you would just send your bank details to whoever," Long said.

"God, yes, I remember those. And apparently quite a few people fell for it. Unbelievable," Hays said.

"Yes, these days things are a lot more sophisticated. But still the thieves harvest millions of euros every year from unsuspecting folks who quite gladly part with their personal details. It amazes me. It's far too easy, but I guess there's no law against being stupid, unfortunately," Wallace said.

"Where is it all coming from?" Lyons asked.

"All over. Not so much from the USA, but lots from Eastern Europe. That's one of the problems. Even when we identify the scammers, it's very difficult to get a conviction. The best you can do is have all their equipment seized, but they're back up and running a week later. I think the technology companies have a lot to answer for. They could be much more protective of their customers. And don't get me started on data breaches," Long said.

"One of the things I'd like to see is the elimination of pay-as-you-go phones," Lyons said. "They are a bloody menace. I can't understand why the airtime providers don't insist on some basic details when they sell a SIM card, it's madness."

"I agree. We're trying to get something done about that, but it's not easy. A good few of the companies selling those SIMs aren't even based in Ireland, so legislation, except on a Europe-wide basis, would be useless. But we still have tricks up our sleeves that catch a few of them out all the same," Wallace said.

As the meal progressed, and the wine lubricated the conversation a bit more, the group continued to exchange theories and stories about their work, until they had finished dessert and coffee, and the waiting staff in the restaurant started clearing tables and making it clear, in a subtle way, that they would like them to leave.

"I'll go and get the car. It's gone a bit chilly out. I'll see you downstairs in a few minutes," Hays said.

They dropped Wallace and Long off at the door of the Imperial, and set off for their own place out in Salthill.

"How do you think that went?" Hays said to Lyons.

"They're quite nice. I was a bit rude to Wallace initially, but he seems to have got over it. Do you think they're at it?"

"What! Two colleagues in An Garda Síochána an item. Whatever next!" he said, reaching across and holding Lyons' hand, giving it an affectionate squeeze.

Chapter Twenty-two

Lyons rose early the following day. The significant amount of wine that she had consumed the previous night appeared to be having no ill effects. "That's what you get when you drink good wine," she said to herself as she showered and prepared for the day ahead. Before parting company with the two detectives from the Fraud Squad the previous evening, they had agreed to travel separately to Clifden, as they were unsure of how long each of their separate missions would take, and Lyons didn't want to be left hanging around waiting on Wallace and Long to finish with the librarian.

It was a pleasant enough day as she said goodbye to Hays who was still enjoying breakfast. It was neither warm not cold, and while there were some ominous-looking clouds overhead, they were high up in the sky, so Lyons figured that she might avoid any serious rainfall on her journey. As it happened, she did encounter a brief shower as she left Moycullen behind her, but by the time she got to Oughterard, the sun had appeared and the remainder of the drive was delightful. Lyons loved the rugged scenery on the road from Oughterard into Clifden. She never tired of the lakes, the heathland all set to the backdrop of the

Partry Mountains out beyond Clonbur. Further on past Recess the Twelve Bens looked magnificent in their sun-bathed blueness. Lyons arrived in Clifden feeling refreshed from the journey and pulled up outside the Garda station.

"Good morning, Séan," she said to Mulholland who was leaning over the counter at the front of the open area reading the paper.

"Ah, 'tis yourself, Maureen. Can I get you a cup of tea, the kettle has just boiled?"

"Thanks, Séan, yes please. It's a lovely day out here. Sometimes I envy the peace and calm you have, Séan."

"Except for the murders, I suppose," Mulholland said.

"Well, there is that. Any more news?"

"No, nothing new. Are you going to call on Bridget O'Toole?"

"Yes, and I was hoping you'd come with me as well," Lyons said.

"Fair enough. But let's have our tea first, then we'll stroll on down to the post office. She'll not be too busy today."

Mulholland produced the two mugs of tea and an opened packet of chocolate Goldgrain biscuits, half-finished. He seemed to have an endless supply of the tasty snack.

When they had finished their refreshments, Mulholland put on his peaked cap, and the two of them set off for the post office a short distance away. They walked past Ann Sweeney's house which still had blue and white Garda tape across the door.

As predicted, the post office was empty, and there was no sign of Bridget O'Toole as Mulholland and Lyons entered the small shop. But the tinkle of the little bell over the door had alerted the postmistress, and she soon appeared from the back of the premises carrying her own mug of tea.

"Good morning, Séan, Inspector. What can I do for you today?" she said, taking up her position behind the glass screen that protected the inner workings of the operation from the public.

"I have a photograph I'd like you to look at, Mrs O'Toole," Lyons said, taking the folded image out of her jacket pocket.

"Call me Bridget, Inspector. No one calls me Mrs O'Toole anymore, not since my husband died, and that's ten years since."

"Oh, sorry, yes, well can you tell me, Bridget, if you have ever seen this man before?"

Bridget took the photograph through the opening in the glass screen and put on her spectacles.

"I have, to be sure. Wasn't he in here looking for Ann Sweeney's house a while back?"

"Are you sure this is the same man, Bridget?" Lyons asked.

"I am, of course. I may need glasses, Inspector, but I'm not blind. That's him."

"Yes, of course, I'm sorry, but we have to be sure. Can you recall exactly when he was in here and what he wanted?"

"Let me see now, it was a few days before that terrible thing that happened. He was only in for a few minutes. He had a parcel under his arm. You know one of those like the courier companies use wrapped in grey plastic."

"What size was this package, Bridget?"

"Wait till we see now. I'd say about the size of two paperback books. Yes, that was it. I remember thinking, when he asked for the Sweeney house, that Ann must be getting more books. Not that she needed any more. The place was stuffed with them already."

"I don't suppose he said where they were coming from?" Lyons asked.

"No, he didn't. And I'm not one to pry into other people's business. What do you take me for?" Bridget said indignantly.

Mulholland cast a glance at Lyons, signalling that he felt they should leave it at that. He was more alert to Bridget's sensitivities than Lyons.

"OK, Bridget. Thanks very much. You have been very helpful. Sorry to have taken so much of your time," Lyons said, keen to placate the woman.

"You're welcome, Inspector. Anytime."

Mulholland and Lyons left the post office and walked back towards the Garda station.

"What do you think now, Maureen?"

"Well, that gives some credence to Paul Wallace's theory. He reckons the courier guy did for Ann, but I'm not so sure. But it does place him in the area at the time of the murder, so I guess we'll have to take it seriously. Tell me, what do you know of the librarian here? Angela McCabe I think her name is."

"Oh, that one. She caused quite a stir when she arrived here a few years back. She's from Limerick, you know," Mulholland said, as if that was enough to convict the woman of some heinous crime in its own right.

"Yes, Adare, I think. What was the issue?"

"She had been here on holiday before she came to live here and set her cap at one of the locals. You can see by the looks of her, he didn't stand much of a chance. But the thing is he was already going out with a grand wee lass from the town here, and everyone thought they would marry. She's the daughter of the people that run the hotel down by the harbour. Anyway, yer man ditched poor Máiréad, and next thing you know McCabe is back and the two of them are getting married. Some folks have never forgiven her."

"I see. And would people really bear a grudge after all this time, Séan?"

"Oh, some would for sure, and I don't think Máiréad ever got over it. She moved away to the city after rather than have to look at the two of them playing happy families. But it's all settled down now. McCabe is quite a nice person really and she helps the old people from the town with lots of stuff. She's more accepted these days."

By this time the two of them were back at the Garda station.

"Are you coming in, Maureen?"

"No, thanks, Séan. I better get back to town. But if you hear anything more about any of this, please let me know immediately. We're struggling a bit with the whole thing."

"I will to be sure. But don't worry lass, you'll get to the bottom of it sooner or later. You always do."

"I hope so, Séan, I really do. See you, and thanks for the tea," Lyons said.

Mulholland just waved as Lyons got back into her car and set off along the N59 back to Galway. She didn't want Wallace to be right about Pavel Berisha, but it was beginning to look like he was.

Chapter Twenty-three

Inspector Paul Wallace and Detective Sergeant Ciara Long arrived out to Clifden in time for the library opening time of half past ten. Wallace was a little curious as to why Lyons had chosen not to travel with them, but he didn't pursue the matter with her. "They have their own way of doing things out here," he said to himself.

They pulled up more or less in front of the library, and Ciara Long walked off a little way down the street to a parking ticket machine armed with a €2 coin. She was surprised to find that parking charges didn't start in Clifden until eleven o'clock, but just in case they hadn't finished talking to Angela McCabe by that time, she bought a ticket anyway and fixed it to the windscreen of Wallace's car.

When they went inside, a very striking-looking woman with a trim figure and long, shiny auburn hair was seated behind the desk looking into a PC screen. She looked up when the two detectives entered.

"Good morning," Wallace said, "we're looking to speak with Angela McCabe."

"That's me. How can I help?"

Wallace introduced the two of them, holding up his warrant card to confirm his identity.

"This will be about poor Ann, I suppose. I've already spoken to another detective from Galway about this. I don't know if there's anything more I can tell you," McCabe said.

"Well, we won't keep you long, Ms McCabe. It's just that some more information has come to light, and we need to check a few things. May I ask if you were in any way involved in Ann Sweeney's business affairs?"

"And what business would that be, Inspector?"

"Mrs Sweeney was dealing in rare books. She acquired and sold first editions on the web. She had quite a good thing going from what we can see. Were you not aware of that at all?"

"No, no I wasn't. Why would I be? She was only a part-time worker here, after all."

"Yes, but presumably you were quite close, and you must have talked quite a bit about things, especially books, is that not right?"

"Are you accusing me of something, Inspector?" Angela McCabe said.

Ciara Long realised that this wasn't getting them anywhere, so she decided to intervene.

"Look, Angela, you don't mind if I call you Angela?" Long said. "A woman has been killed. We don't think it was a random occurrence, so we're just investigating the circumstances, that's all. We're not accusing anyone of anything, but there are some emails on Ann's laptop that indicate you may know something about her business."

"What sort of emails?" McCabe said.

"Perhaps it would be best if you just tell us exactly what you know. We'd rather not have to get you to close up here and come to the local Garda station with us."

Angela McCabe stared at Ciara Long for what seemed like an age.

"Very well, I'll tell you. I did give Ann some help in identifying books that could be of value. We sorted through the donations together, and sometimes, not often, we'd come across a book that had some value due to its rarity. Ann would take those away, but I don't know what happened after that. I doubt she made a fortune out of it, and I did nothing illegal. The books didn't belong to the library or anything."

"I see. And what did you get out of it, Angela?"

"Me? Nothing. I just wanted to give her a bit of a hand with things. That husband of hers is a right skinflint, and she had Dónal to support."

"And you're sure you didn't profit by this little enterprise in any way at all?"

"Certain, yes. Don't you believe me?"

"Perhaps. But I'd like permission from you to access your bank account records, just to be certain, if that's OK?" Wallace said, re-joining the conversation.

"I don't think so, Inspector. I'd like to consult a solicitor before this gets too silly for words," McCabe said, reddening a little.

"Very well. That's your prerogative. But it does tend to leave the impression that you may have something to hide, and that just makes us dig a little deeper. It's up to you," Wallace said. "We'll leave it for now to give you a chance to consult a solicitor, but we will be back in touch in a few days. Meanwhile, if you change your mind, here's my phone number," he said, handing the woman a business card.

The two of them left the library. Outside it was turning into a nice day, and Wallace said to his colleague, "Fancy a coffee before we head back to town?"

"Yes, please. Let's walk on down the street and find a cafe. The car is paid up for a good while yet."

After a few minutes strolling down along Market Street they came to Walsh's bakery where the inviting smell of freshly baked bread and coffee was wafting out onto the footpath.

Inside, they got the last available free table, and as they sat down, a woman came across to take their order. They both opted for coffee and a Danish pastry.

"What did you think of that, then?" Wallace said.

"Well, I'd say she's been at it with Sweeney at some level. But I don't reckon her for the brains behind the whole thing, do you?" Long said.

"No, probably not. She was quick enough to look for a lawyer though. There must be something going on. Of course, there is a way we could find out," Wallace said.

"Oh yes? What's that then?"

"Let's say there was a donation of books to the library, maybe from a deceased estate or something. We could plant a valuable book in with that lot that has a tracker in it. They can make these things very small, and it could easily be hidden in the binding along the spine. What do you think?"

"Cripes! Sounds a bit sci-fi to me, but maybe, if we can't get any further any other way, it could be useful. Would it take long to arrange?" Long said.

"The impossible we can do at once. Miracles take a bit longer!" Wallace said.

Chapter Twenty-four

Eamon Flynn brought Mary Costelloe along with him to see Ann Sweeney's husband at his builder's yard. They wanted to ask him about the last time he had seen the 20-bore shotgun that they believed was used to kill the woman.

Flynn swung his car into the yard, and was pleased to see that Sweeney's vehicle was parked outside the makeshift office. The two detectives got out and Flynn went inside.

"Good morning, Mr Sweeney," Flynn said, "I'd like to have another word with you if you could spare me a few minutes. It won't take long."

"It better not, I'm very busy today. What do you want?" the man said gruffly.

"Last time we spoke, you told us that your son went back to your house after you had both been out shooting rabbits, and that he had put his gun, along with your 12-bore back in the gun cabinet at your home. Is that right?"

"Yes. That's correct. Why? Do you not believe me?"

"Well, it's just that your story doesn't agree with what Dónal has told us," Flynn said and let the sentence hang in the air.

"Why? What did he say?"

"He told us that he kept the gun in the car, and that sometime later when it was parked up, the car was broken into and the gun stolen from under a rug in the back seat."

Sweeney looked down at his boots.

"Look, maybe I made a mistake. All I can say is that usually, that's what happens. Dónal is quite fussy about security, and he always goes through the same procedure when we've been out shooting. Maybe my recollection is wrong. I'm sorry, I didn't mean to mislead you."

"That's not very satisfactory, given what happened, Mr Sweeney. I'll have to ask you to call into the station and amend your statement. Would tomorrow morning suit?" Flynn said.

"I guess. But does this mean Dónal is in trouble?" Sweeney said.

"Our investigation is continuing, Mr Sweeney, but it's not helpful when we get inaccurate information. Let's leave it at that for now, but I'd like to see you at 10:00 a.m. tomorrow to try and get this sorted out."

While Flynn had gone into the office to talk to Conan Sweeney, Mary Costelloe remained outside and went for a wander around the yard. She walked around the back of the office building where there was quite a lot of rubbish scattered around. Behind a pile of scaffolding poles and boards, she saw an old blue oil barrel that was raised up on some concrete blocks that looked as if it had been used to burn stuff. She went across and peered into the barrel, but there was just a lot of charred ash left in the base of it. Beside the old barrel there were two black plastic sacks standing upright. Mary's curiosity was piqued, so she opened one of the bags and looked inside. The bag was full of paper waste. The long strips of whitish-coloured paper had no writing or printing on it, and it wasn't the right shape for wallpaper trimmings, or anything else she could recognise. She couldn't see why a builder would have such material for burning, so she dipped into the

nearest bag and collected one or two of the paper strips
and placed them into a clear plastic bag before putting
them back in her pocket.

When she walked back to the front of the office, Flynn
was waiting outside for her.

"Ready?" he said.

"Yes, sorry, I was just having a snoop around."

"Find anything of interest?" Flynn said.

"Maybe."

As they sat into the car, Mary Costelloe produced the
plastic bag with the paper strips inside.

"I picked up these around the back."

"What are they?" Flynn asked.

"I'm not sure, but they looked out of place, and I'm a
curious girl, so I'll take them back and let Sinéad have a
look at them."

"Hmm... OK. I'm not sure that's going to help us to
solve the murder though."

"Probably not, but I have a feeling about these. Call it
women's intuition."

"God, spare us!" Flynn said, smirking.

* * *

When they got back to the station, Mary Costelloe went
off in search of Sinéad Loughran, while Flynn sought out
Lyons.

"Hi, Eamon. Well, what's the story?" she said.

"Story is right. I think we need to talk to Dónal again.
There's something not right going on here, and it seems to
involve the young lad," Flynn said.

"Oh. What's that?"

Flynn went on to tell Lyons how Sweeney had
dismissed the divergence in the stories between Dónal and
his father, and hadn't provided him a satisfactory
explanation for it.

"Hmm... you're right, there's something fishy going on.
I think I'll get Sally to go and have another word with him

122

tomorrow morning. She seems to get on his wavelength. Maybe she can find out what's what."

"Good idea. Any news on the CCTV footage from Recess?"

"Nothing good. John sent it up to Dublin, but they weren't able to do much with it. All they could say is that it looks like a car going at speed towards Clifden and then coming back about forty-five minutes later. But they couldn't get any details of the make and model, or the registration."

"Bugger. That's no use then. Any other leads developing?" Flynn said.

"Well, I've still to talk to Inspector Wallace and Ciara Long about whatever they discovered talking to the librarian out in Clifden, but that's about it, I'm afraid. I'm going to have to go upstairs and brief the Super shortly, and he won't be best pleased with our lack of progress," Lyons said.

* * *

Detective Superintendent Mick Hays was busy with one of his tiresome reports that seemed to occupy most of his time when Lyons knocked at his door.

"Oh, hi. Come in. I could do with a little light relief from this lot. What have you got?"

"Not a lot, to be truthful. But I thought I'd better let you know how it's going anyway," she said taking a seat in front of his desk.

"Remind me again what it's all about," Hays said.

"It's this shooting out in Clifden. You know, the separated woman with the dodgy books and the son at UCG. And of course, we still have the two super sleuths from Dublin hanging around too."

"Are they being any help at all?"

"They're not in the way, but that's about it. But they are being nice enough about things. It's just they have different objectives to us. They're all tied up in this fraudulent printing crap. I have a murderer to catch! Don't suppose you have any ideas, have you?"

Hays leaned back in his chair, now thoroughly distracted from his own work.

"Have you followed the money trail?"

"We have, not that it's told us much. There's a good bit of it sloshing around, but it's proving very hard to track properly beyond Mrs Sweeney's bank account in Utrecht. I'm sure there's more there to be discovered, it's just getting at the information that's the problem."

"Can Wallace not help out with that? He should have some great contacts in Europe."

"I could ask him, I suppose. But is that going to get us any closer to the killer?" Lyons said.

"I'm not sure what to suggest, love. If you like I could sit in on your evening briefing, if you think I could add any value?"

"Have you got the time?" Lyons said.

"For you, always," he said, smiling broadly.

"OK. You're on. Say five o'clock downstairs. See you then."

* * *

The team came together later in the afternoon. Hays had come down from on high, and stood at the back of the open plan while Lyons got the meeting underway.

"OK, everyone. Let's compare notes. Can I start with you, Paul?"

Wallace relayed the discussion that they had with Angela McCabe in the library in Clifden.

"So, what you're saying is that she was in cahoots with Ann Sweeney in some way concerning the side-lining of some valuable books?" Lyons said.

"Looks that way, but as soon as we began to probe her a bit she started talking about solicitors. So, we said we'd get back to her."

"OK. I think you should follow that up sooner rather than later, though. Would you agree?"

"Yes, I suppose so. Maybe we'll call her tomorrow," Wallace said.

Lyons then briefed the group on the fruitless efforts with the CCTV footage from Recess. Just as she was finishing with the bad news, Mary Costelloe came in, a little out of breath, and took a seat beside Eamon Flynn.

"All right, Mary? Anything to share with us?" Lyons said, clearly a little miffed at the late arrival of the girl.

Costelloe blushed, but went on to say, "Yes, Inspector. When we were out at Mr Sweeney's place earlier, I came across some odd-looking waste paper that he appeared to be burning at the back of his office building. I took a few pieces over to Sinéad Loughran. That's why I was late – sorry."

"And?" Lyons said.

"Sinéad says the paper is the kind that is used to make banknotes. It's very high quality, and probably came off large sheets of some kind. She said it's very difficult to get hold of the right stuff, and she had no explanation as to why a builder would have any of it anywhere in his possession. And if you recall, Inspector Flynn, when we were out there before, Sweeney came back into the yard with a truck, and there was a stack of MDF sheets on the back of the lorry."

"Yes, now that you mention it. He said it was something to do with a job over near Clongowna."

"Crikey! What does anyone make of that?" Lyons said.

"It looks to me as if Mr Sweeney may be involved in the forged euro notes that we were talking about before. Maybe he cuts up the big sheets and moves the forged currency on to the next link in the chain," Paul Wallace said, "and we have evidence to suggest that there is a connection between the forged €50 notes and the forged first editions too."

There was silence in the room while the group digested this new and somewhat surprising development.

Hays raised his hand at the back of the room and caught Lyons' attention.

"Yes, Superintendent," she said.

Hays made his way to the front of the little group.

"If I'm reading this correctly then, we have a small cluster of suspects all connected to a number of criminal enterprises involving counterfeit money, forged books and God knows what else. Who are the key players?" he said.

"Well, there's Ann Sweeney, her husband, possibly the library woman, McCabe, and maybe the son, Dónal, is involved in some way too," Lyons said.

"And don't forget Pavel Berisha," Wallace added.

"But which one of this lot had a clear motive for murder?" Hays said.

"We haven't enough information yet, but my money is on the husband," Eamon Flynn said.

"I'm not so sure. There's a big fat gap in the son's story about the gun. I think Sally should go out to Moyola again in the morning and see if she can get anything more from him," Lyons said, looking at Sally Fahy.

"Do you think it's OK for her to go on her own?" Hays said.

"Yes, I do. If we go in mob-handed we'll get nothing out of him. He's scared enough of the police as it is. Let Sally handle it. She has a way with the lad. Are you OK with that, Sally?"

"Yes, of course, boss. I'll hit the place first thing. Surprise him a bit."

"I'd like to mount an operation on Sweeney's yard too," Wallace said.

"Maybe you could hold off on that, Paul, till we see what Sally gets. He's not going anywhere after all. Anyway, it will take you a while to set it up properly."

"Yes, OK. I'll get working on it in the morning then, and be ready to pounce once Sally's finished with Dónal."

Chapter Twenty-five

Sally Fahy drove out to Moyola Park at ten o'clock the following morning. She reckoned that that could be interpreted as 'first thing' for students, and she wasn't wrong. When she had parked in the usual spot a few doors down from number 23, she went to the dingy front door and knocked firmly. The place reminded her of the accommodation she had occupied when she herself was a student at college in Cork. She had studied Sociology for three years, and in her final year saw an advertisement in *The Irish Examiner* for the Garda Síochána. It was at a time when the government of the day were doing their best to enrol female recruits, and with a promising result in her degree coming up, she breezed through the entrance exam with ease.

There was no reply at the door, so Fahy knocked harder the second time, and stood back to wait. After a few minutes a shape appeared in the glass, and the door was opened a little by a thin young man in boxer shorts with wild unkempt hair.

"What the fuck do you want?" he croaked, not being best pleased to be awoken at such an early time of day.

"I need to see Dónal. Is he in, please?" Fahy said, ignoring the lad's less than enthusiastic greeting.

The lad said nothing, but opened the door wider which Fahy took to be an invitation to enter the premises.

The young man roared up the stairs, "Dónal. It's your girlfriend from the police. Get your arse down here."

Fahy waited a little impatiently for what seemed like an age, and just when she was about to go and get the same young man back out of his pit, a door opened at the top of the stairs, and Dónal Sweeney emerged dressed in blue denim jeans and a black sweatshirt. When he got to the foot of the stairs, he greeted Fahy and gestured towards the kitchen at the back of the house, which he was certain would be unoccupied at that time of the morning. The other young man went back upstairs, presumably to continue his slumber.

When the two were seated at the table, Fahy said, "Dónal, we are concerned about the different stories that have been given to us about the shotgun. Your father insists that you put it back in the gun cabinet at his house the last time it was used, but you told us that it was stolen from the back of your car. Which is it?"

"Stay here a minute, I'll be right back."

Dónal got up and left the room, leaving Fahy wondering what exactly was going on. She didn't have long to wait. Dónal was back, and he had a shotgun in his hands pointed directly at her.

"Is that the same gun?" Sally said as coolly as she could manage.

"What do you think?" Sweeney said.

"OK. So why don't you put it down, Dónal, and we can talk about it?"

"There's been enough talk. Too much, really. I've had enough talk to do me a lifetime. Now put your hands where I can see them on the table," he said, still pointing the weapon at Fahy's midriff.

Fahy did as she was told.

"Is that thing loaded?" Fahy said.

"Damn right!"

"OK. So, what do you want to happen next, Dónal?"

"You're going to get me safe passage out of here, that's what."

Just then, Fahy's phone started ringing in her pocket.

"Who's that?" Sweeney said nervously, raising the gun and pointing it straight at the detective.

"It's my boss. I'll have to take it, or she'll know there's something wrong."

"OK. But just say we're talking. Don't say anything else or I'll have to use this thing on you."

Fahy took the phone slowly out of her pocket and answered the call.

"Hello, Inspector. What's up?"

"Hi, Sally. Just wondering where you are?"

"I'm here with Dónal Sweeney at his place in Moyola Park. We're just having a chat about the gun. Did you want me for something?"

"No, sorry. I'd forgotten that's where you were going this morning. That's fine. See you later."

"Yeah, see you."

Fahy put the phone back in her pocket, but she didn't hang up, so the line was left open. She hoped Maureen Lyons would be smart enough to pick up the conversation that followed.

"So, are you planning to kill me, Dónal?"

"That depends on you. Now you need to get making those arrangements."

"What exactly do you want me to do, Dónal? And I'd feel a whole lot more comfortable if you'd just put that gun down."

"Don't be stupid. Now get onto whoever. I want a private plane at Galway Airport. We'll be flying to Langeveld. It's a small airfield west of Amsterdam. I can arrange to be met there. Oh, and by the way, you're coming with me!"

* * *

Lyons continued to listen to the conversation between Sweeney and her Detective Sergeant after she had said goodbye to Fahy. After a few minutes the phone went dead, but she had heard enough.

She went out into the open plan and summoned Eamon Flynn and Mary Costelloe, and while she was waiting for them to come into her office, she called Mick Hays on the phone.

"Mick, it's me. We have a problem. Sally is out at Moyola Park with Dónal Sweeney, and he's holding her at gunpoint."

"Jesus! Are you serious? OK. I'm coming down. Get onto Pat Mulgrew in the Armed Response Unit and give him the details. I'll see you in a sec."

Lyons waved Flynn and Costelloe into the room as she called the head of the ARU.

"Pat, it's Maureen Lyons. We have a hostage situation out at Moyola Park. My sergeant, Sally Fahy, is being held at gunpoint by a student called Dónal Sweeney. It's number 23. Can you get ready to roll? I think Superintendent Hays is going to take charge."

"Yes, sure, Maureen. We'll be downstairs, all tooled up in ten minutes."

"Great. See you then."

* * *

Inside the house at Moyola Park, Sally Fahy was thinking quickly. She knew that Sweeney's plan for a safe passage out of the country was a non-starter, but she didn't want to tell him that for obvious reasons.

"Dónal, what's all this about? Did you have anything to do with your mother's death?"

"Shut up! Just concentrate on getting us out of here, and do as I say. Who is your superior officer? I mean the big cheese – not Lyons."

"That would be Superintendent Hays. He's in overall charge of the detective unit."

"Right. Well, give him a call and tell him to organise a plane out at the airport to take me to Langeveld, and I want it in an hour, no bullshit!"

"Listen, Dónal, you can't possibly hope to take a gun on an aircraft. It just doesn't make any sense. Why don't you give yourself in, and we can talk about whatever's bothering you?" Fahy said.

"Look, don't piss me about," he said, lifting the gun up to his shoulder and pointing it directly at Fahy's head, "just do what I say or you'll be sorry."

"OK, OK. Keep your hair on," Fahy said, taking her phone out of her pocket and deftly making sure the call to Lyons wasn't still transmitting.

* * *

The sound of several sirens cutting through the calm morning air resounded throughout Moyola Park. Hays' car, and two brightly coloured BMW jeeps with Armed Response Unit painted on their front door drew to a halt outside number 23 with their blue and red lights flashing. As they all got out of their vehicles, an upstairs window in the house was flung open and a scruffy-looking youth looked out and shouted, "What the fuck is going on?"

Hays, clad in a bulletproof vest and sporting a black baseball cap with the word 'Garda' embroidered into it, stepped in a bit closer to the property and said, "What's your name?"

"Todd. But what's happening?"

"Your mate Dónal is holding one of our officers at gunpoint. So, stay in your room. Don't attempt to film what's going on, that's an offence, and stay off social media. Is there a back entrance to the house?"

"Yes, there is. There's a lane along the side of number 27 and you can get to the back of the house that way," Todd said.

"Right. Stay in your room with the door closed. We'll let you know when it's all clear."

Hays turned away and went back to the footpath where by now four ARU officers were assembled with their Heckler & Koch HK416 assault rifles at the ready.

"Right, I'm taking charge, so you only take instructions from me, unless I am wounded, in which case Senior Inspector Lyons will take over. Understood?"

The men all agreed.

"OK. Radio check."

The four armed Gardaí blipped their radios in turn, and Hays could hear the transmission on the unit fixed to his armoured vest.

"Good. Now, two of you round the back. See if you can get the gunman in your sights, but no shooting unless someone is in imminent danger of being killed. And check with me before discharging your weapons. Got it?"

"Yes, sir," the men replied in unison. With that, two of them peeled off and trotted down towards the lane in a semi-crouched position.

"Right. You two, line up close to the front door, one either side. Same goes for you. No shooting unless it looks like someone is about to be shot, and wait for my order. Clear?"

"Yes, sir," they said, and went up to the front of the house to stand either side of the entrance.

Lyons, who had been standing off while her partner set things up, came over.

"What do you want me to do, Mick?"

"I want you to establish contact with yer man. Let's see if we can get Sally out of there without anyone getting hurt. You OK with that?"

"Yes, sure. I'll call Sally's mobile now."

Chapter Twenty-six

"What's all that noise?" Dónal Sweeney said to Sally Fahy in the kitchen of the little house.

"That will be the Armed Response Unit, Dónal. You know, you really should give this up now before someone gets hurt. These guys don't mess around, especially as you're holding one of their own at gunpoint. You're quite likely to get shot in the head."

"Shut up, bitch! I've told you. We're going to fly out of here."

Fahy could see that the young man was getting very agitated. In these situations, or so she had been told during training, there comes a time when the person with the gun realises that there in a hopeless position, and that their demands are not being met. That's when they are at their most dangerous as, from that time on, they have little to lose.

Just then, Sally Fahy's phone started ringing.

"Answer it," Sweeney barked.

"Hi, Sally. This is Maureen. Can I speak to Dónal please?"

Fahy held up the phone towards her captor.

"It's for you," she said. She thought that if Sweeney had to take the phone in one hand she might catch him off balance and be able to disarm him. But it was risky. She could get shot for her trouble.

"Put it on speaker on the table," Sweeney said, alert to the situation.

"Hello, Dónal. This is Senior Inspector Maureen Lyons. Is everyone all right in there?"

"Have you got the plane arranged?"

"We're working on that now, Dónal. There isn't one that can fly to the Netherlands actually at Galway Airport, so they're having to get one in from Cork. It will be a couple of hours before the preparations are complete."

"Fuck!" he shouted, and then in a slightly more relaxed tone, "OK. Well, we're staying here till it's ready, then I want a van to take us to the airport. I can't fit this bloody gun in a saloon car. Got it?"

"Yes, that won't be a problem, Dónal. But you should know that your house is surrounded by armed Gardaí now, and if they see you make any move to hurt our officer, they have orders to shoot. Do you understand?"

Sweeney looked out the back window, but could see nothing untoward in the yard.

"Yes, right. You're bluffing, you sad cow. There's no one there."

* * *

Hays' radio crackled into life.

"Three here, sir. I'm on the roof of the garage behind number twenty-five. I have clear sight of the gunman. I can take a head shot if you like?"

"Negative, three. But keep him in your sights, and if he makes any moves on Fahy, call me at once."

"Roger that, sir."

* * *

Inside the house, Sally Fahy was using all her experience to try and improve the situation.

"Dónal, why don't you put that thing down. It must be heavy holding it up all the time like that."

"Yeah, right. No chance," he said, brandishing the weapon.

"OK, well at least let me get you a cup of tea."

"Yeah, OK. I'm parched actually."

Sally got up and filled the rather dirty cream-coloured kettle from the cold tap and put it on to boil.

"The tea bags are in the cupboard over the sink, and the spoons are in the drawer," Sweeney said.

Sally took two tea bags and put one each into rather badly stained mugs that at least had been recently washed. She opened the cutlery drawer. Inside, teaspoons were arranged at the front and to the right there was a selection of what looked like quite sharp kitchen knives. Making sure that her body was between Sweeney and the cutlery, she slipped one of the knives up her sleeve. She then poured the boiling water into the mugs, went to the fridge and got some milk, and put the whole lot on the kitchen table.

* * *

After another half hour, Lyons was getting restless, so she walked over to where Hays was standing.

"What are we going to do next, Mick?"

"We're going to end this thing. I want you to call them again and tell them we have the plane arranged. If he asks about the van, tell him it's down the road. I want to get them to come out, but give me a few minutes."

"OK."

Hays then got on his radio.

"Three and four. You can come back to the front of the house now and take cover down behind the cars, but keep your weapons pointed to the front door. Acknowledge."

"Roger, sir. On our way."

A couple of minutes later the two ARU officers came crouching along in front of the houses, staying out of sight below the garden walls.

Hays told the four ARU officers to point their weapons at the front of the house.

"When Sweeney comes out, see if you can get a shot into his leg or even his arm. But wait for my signal. Understood?"

"Yes, sir," they said in unison.

Hays gave a thumbs-up signal to Lyons.

She called Sally Fahy's phone again.

"Hi, Sally. Put the phone on loudspeaker, would you?"

Lyons heard the slight echo that was generated as the phone went to speaker mode.

"OK, Dónal, we have the plane ready now. So, you need to come out nice and slowly through the front door," Lyons said.

"Neat. OK. We're coming out. No tricks now."

"Of course not."

The Gardaí could see the shadow of Sally Fahy's uniform appearing in the glass of the hall door. It opened slowly, and Sally emerged onto the front step. Dónal Sweeney could be seen behind her, and it looked as if he had the shotgun lodged in the back of her uniform.

Fahy came out a bit further, and soon Sweeney was out in the open, away from the cover of the entrance. As he stepped down onto the concrete in front of the house, suddenly the upstairs window opened and Todd leaned out and yelled, "Watch out, Dónal, they have guns. They'll fucking kill you!"

Sweeney was distracted. He looked up to where his mate was hanging out of the window, and as he turned his head, the gun pointed up and away from Fahy's back. She saw her chance. She took the knife down from where she had concealed it earlier, pirouetted around, and lunged at

Sweeney, stabbing him deeply in the biceps of the arm he was using to hold the gun.

Sweeney screamed in agony, dropping the gun, which clattered to the ground, discharging a round as it fell, smashing the side windows of his car parked in the driveway. He fell to the ground, clutching his bleeding arm and yelping in pain.

Two of the ARU officers ran in and pointed their weapons at Sweeney's head. "Down, stay down," they shouted.

Another walked in slowly, and picked up the shotgun. He broke the weapon and removed the remaining live cartridge. Then he separated both halves of the gun, holding them up and shouting, "Weapon secured."

When Lyons heard this, she dashed across and wrapped Sally Fahy in her arms. Fahy was still holding the kitchen knife in her hand which was dripping blood onto the ground, so Lyons took it and placed it in a plastic evidence bag.

"Jesus, Sally, are you OK?"

"Yes, boss. A bit shook. But I'm not hurt."

Lyons, still with her arm around her colleague, walked them both slowly back to the footpath, and sat Sally Fahy into one of the Garda cars.

As soon as Hays heard that the shotgun was secured, he called in the ambulance that had been standing off in case it was needed. Two paramedics jumped out and started attending to Dónal Sweeney who was still bleeding profusely. They staunched the bleeding, helped him to his feet, and supported him back to the ambulance where two uniformed Gardaí joined him. Before it set off for the hospital with sirens blaring and blue lights flashing, Hays read the man his rights and arrested him for assaulting a police officer and illegal detention of a Garda.

As the ambulance disappeared, Hays walked over to where the lead ARU officer was debriefing his men.

"Thanks for that. A great piece of work. Thank the lads for me too," Hays said.

"Christ, that young blonde girl has some balls. I wouldn't like to tackle her on a dark night," the man said.

"We make 'em tough in the Detective Unit. You should see some of the things her boss gets up to."

"I'd rather not, thanks. Anyway, glad it ended well for everyone."

"Me too. Tell the lads there'll be a pint in Doherty's for them later. And thanks again."

"Thanks, Superintendent," the man said, as he went to officially stand down his team and secure their weapons, placing them back in the lock-boxes in their vehicles.

Hays went over to the squad car where Fahy and Lyons were sitting. He leant his arm on the roof, and bent down to talk to them through the open window.

"Are you OK, Sally? Do you need to go to hospital for a check-up?" he said.

"No thanks, sir, I'm grand. But I could do with a strong drink."

"I'll bet! Maureen, can you look after that for us. It's on me."

"Sure. What about Sweeney?" Lyons said.

"Ah, don't worry. I'll tidy that up after I've had a word with his pal upstairs. I want to see if he's been making movies on his phone."

"Oh, OK. See you a bit later then."

Lyons closed the window of the car, and the uniformed Garda driver set off towards the city.

Chapter Twenty-seven

Inspector Paul Wallace was getting ready for a mission of his own. He spoke to Eamon Flynn, who was only too glad to get involved, having been left out of the action at Dónal Sweeney's house. They equipped themselves with a search warrant, collected four uniformed Gardaí, and set off in convoy for Conan Sweeney's yard.

Light rain was beginning to fall as they drove out towards Ballinasloe. That's how it usually started, but Flynn was sure it would be a downpour before long, and that wouldn't make their job any easier once they arrived.

Sweeney's Mercedes was parked in front of the makeshift office and as they all got out of their respective vehicles, Sweeney came out to greet them, looking surprised.

Wallace approached him. "Good day, Mr Sweeney. I have here a warrant to search this entire premises and any vehicles that are here too. It's all in order if you'd like to examine it," he said, holding out the folded paper for the man.

Sweeney unfolded the paper and scanned it quickly.

"What are you hoping to find, Inspector?" Sweeney said.

"Let's just see, shall we?"

Wallace nodded to the nearest uniformed Garda and two of them entered the office, while more of them went off around the back and into the storage sheds. Sweeney and Wallace stayed outside.

"Look, Inspector, what's all this about? I've already told you all about the shotguns. Do you not believe me?"

"This isn't about guns, Mr Sweeney. It's more serious than that."

Sweeney looked puzzled.

"Well then, are you going to tell me? Because I'm sure I can't imagine what you're after. This is a legitimate building company, all insured, VAT registered and our Tax Clearance Certificate is bang up to date as well as all our payroll taxes. You'll not find anything out of kilter here."

"What do you know about printing, Mr Sweeney?" Wallace said.

"Printing? Me? Nothing at all. What kind of printing are you talking about?"

"Any kind of printing. Books, money, documents, just printing in general."

"Look, Inspector, I'm a builder by trade. Ask me anything you like about walls, floors and roofs, plumbing, heating, tiling – you name it. But I know nothing about any printing."

* * *

Inside the enormous storage shed on the other side of the yard from the offices, the uniformed Gardaí were rummaging through all sorts of materials. There were endless tins of paint, buckets of tile cement, piles of bricks and blocks, roof tiles and floor tiles and various bags of grouting and adhesives all in a rather chaotic arrangement.

As they got towards the back of the shed, behind a rather weather-beaten forklift truck, there was a rolled steel shutter that was very well secured with two big locks going into strong metal eyes on the floor.

Flynn, who was supervising the search, walked over to where two of the Gardaí were trying to open it.

"What's the story, lads?"

"It's locked tight, boss."

"Can you break the locks?" Flynn said.

"We'd have to get some cutting gear in. I don't suppose yer man would give us the key?" the man said.

"Wait here, I'll go and ask him."

Flynn trotted across the yard trying to dodge the worst of the rain and found that Sweeney and Wallace had moved into Wallace's car in an effort to stay dry. Flynn knocked at the window.

"Mr Sweeney, have you got the keys to the roller shutter at the back of the big shed?"

"No, we haven't. That thing hasn't been open for years. I've no idea where the key is."

"Well, in that case, we're going to have to drill out the locks. It would be a lot easier if we had the keys," Flynn said.

"I told you. I don't have them. And you'd better be prepared to make good any damage you cause too. Those locks are expensive, you know."

Flynn said nothing, and trotted back across the yard and into the shed.

"See if you can find an angle grinder, Jim. Yer man says he hasn't got the keys."

"Righto, boss. I'm sure there's one around here somewhere."

It didn't take long for the Garda to locate what he needed, and in a few minutes, he was bent down with protective goggles, cutting at the locks with a stream of sparks flying out onto the concrete floor behind him. Ten minutes later, he had both locks removed and was asking his colleague for help lifting the shutter.

When the room behind the entrance was revealed and the lights had been turned on, a very different spectacle presented itself. Firstly, the room was spotlessly clean –

almost clinically so. Along one wall, steel shelving was arranged, and here and there along its length, cardboard boxes sat, sealed with brown parcel tape.

At the far end of the room, a bench was positioned that occupied about half of the width of the back wall, and beside it was an industrial paper guillotine complete with a wide blade that glistened in the light, a proper safety guard, two foot pedals to operate the thing and a large metal bed on which to rest sizeable stacks of paper ready for cutting. To the right of the machine there were some industrial waste bins into which black plastic sacks had been placed, and Flynn noticed that there were offcuts of paper similar to the ones Mary Costelloe had retrieved from outside, protruding from one of the bins.

In the centre of the room, resting on a wooden pallet, there was a stack of roughly ten sheets of MDF. The black metal straps that had held the pile together had been cut, and were hanging down at the sides.

"Well, well, what have we here?" Flynn said out loud as he examined the scene.

Even though Wallace was not far away, Flynn didn't feel like getting another soaking, so he called his colleague on his mobile phone.

"Paul, you'd better come over to the big shed. We're down the back. We've found something," Flynn said.

"OK, I'll be right there."

Wallace gave Sweeney a sardonic look and got out of the car, being sure to take the ignition keys with him. He sprinted across the yard, and joined Flynn and the others in the back room.

"Wow. Nice work, Eamon," he said, looking around and taking in the picture before him.

Signalling to two of the uniformed Gardaí, Wallace instructed them to take the sheets of MDF down and stack them at an angle against the wall. The material was removed one sheet at a time, but there was nothing found in between the layers, which was a disappointment to Flynn and Wallace.

When all the wood was stacked as Wallace had instructed, he said, "Right. Everyone out. No need to contaminate the scene any further. Two of you stand guard at the front of the shed, and no one, and I mean no one at all, comes in here till forensics have had a good go over the place."

Flynn was on the phone to Sinéad Loughran.

"Hi, Sinéad. I'm out here at Conan Sweeney's builder's yard in Ballinasloe. We need you here to examine a lock-up we've found with some interesting equipment and stuff. Do you think you could come out?"

"Yes, of course, Inspector. Ballinasloe, you say. That will take us about forty minutes I reckon. Have you secured the place to prevent contamination?"

"Yes, as best we can in any case. Thanks, Sinéad. I'll send the co-ordinates to your mobile phone so you can find the place. See you shortly."

Flynn then turned to Wallace.

"What do you want to do now, Paul?"

"We'll take Sweeney back to Galway under caution. I want to let him stew for a while till we find out if we can connect him directly to this lot. Does Loughran have one of those portable fingerprint kits?" Wallace said.

"I think so. Get Sweeney's fingerprints into the system as soon as you can in any case. If she has, then she can do a comparison from here. I'll stay here and supervise the operation. Is that OK?" Flynn said.

"Yes, please, that would be great. I'll see you later."

Chapter Twenty-eight

Loughran's white 4x4 rolled into Sweeney's yard some forty minutes after she had received the call from Flynn. The rain had eased off quite a bit by then, so Flynn walked across to greet her.

"Sorry about that, sir, the traffic was horrendous. A broken-down truck on the R446 when we came off the motorway. So, what have we got?"

"It's over here. We found a workroom behind some roller shutters that had been very well secured with stout locks. I'm afraid we had to cut the locks off. Sweeney said he didn't have the key, which was obviously a lie. Sorry about that."

"Ah, no bother. If it was that well secured, they probably weren't too careful inside. Let me get a couple of the lads in there and we'll see what's what."

"Thanks. We found some sheets of MDF stacked on a pallet too. We lifted them off and stacked them against the wall. I was sure there would be something hidden in between the sheets, but there was nothing, I'm afraid," Flynn said.

"OK. Don't worry. Just let us get on. Are you staying?" Loughran said.

"Yes, but I'll keep out of your way. Wallace has taken Sweeney back to Mill Street, and he's putting his fingerprints into the system."

"Great. OK, let's see what we can find."

Flynn wandered back to the office where the uniformed officers were just finishing up their search of the place.

"Anything of interest, lads?" he said through the open door.

"There's a good lot of paperwork, but it all looks normal enough. There are bank statements which might be of interest, and Sweeney's laptop is here, but it's password-protected," the young Garda said.

"OK. Well, bag up anything you think might be useful, and bring the laptop. John O'Connor will have some fun getting inside that for us."

* * *

A good hour had passed before Sinéad Loughran emerged from the shed with her trusty Nikon camera, complete with a large flash gun dangling from around her neck. She walked over to Flynn's car and sat into the passenger's seat, removing the hood from her white scene-of-crime suit.

"Well, anything?" Flynn said.

"Yes. Lots. Not many fingerprints on the guillotine, but we got a good thumbprint from the steel band that was securing the stack of MDF sheets. I'll compare it to Sweeney's when Wallace gets it into the system."

"Is that it?" Flynn said, trying not to let the disappointment come through too much.

"No, of course not. You didn't check those sheets of MDF very thoroughly, did you?" Loughran said.

"No, we didn't. Wallace was convinced there could be something hidden between the sheets, but there was nothing."

"Ah, but there was! We re-examined the underside of them. On two, we found imprints where something that wasn't quite dry was placed against the stuff. It's quite feint, but I've got some excellent photographs," she said tapping her camera, "and when I get them enhanced back at base, I bet they show images of €50 notes."

"Cool. How certain are you?" Flynn said.

"Oh, I'd say about eighty percent. Is that good enough for you?"

"Excellent. Anything else?"

"Yes, actually. There was a scrunched-up sheet of paper that had fallen down between the laths into the pallet. It's pretty battered, but when I get it back to the lab, I'll probably be able to sort it out. It might tell us where the MDF came from, or at least where it was made."

"That's fantastic, Sinéad. I don't know how you do it."

"Practice, boss, lots and lots of practice. But listen, we need to get that stuff back to Galway. It won't fit in my jeep. Can you make some arrangements? I'll get the lads to put it back on the pallet and wrap it in cling film."

"Yes, OK, I'm sure we can manage that."

Flynn arranged for a truck to come out and collect the stack of MDF sheets, and the odd-looking convoy set off back to Galway. When Loughran got back to her laboratory, she started working on all the evidence that had come in during the day. It was going to be a long night.

* * *

At six o'clock, Lyons brought everyone back together for a meeting.

"Right, let's see what we have between us now."

Lyons filled the group in on the events of the morning at Moyola Park where Sally Fahy had essentially disarmed Dónal Sweeney.

"Dónal Sweeney is in custody now and I've sent Sally home. I think she was more shaken than she was admitting. She may well have thought that her number was up. I know she's tough, but that was a bit much, even for her," Lyons said.

"I'll give her a call later to see if she's OK. Is there anyone at home to look after her, talk things through?" Flynn said.

"Thanks, Eamon. No, I don't think so. But I'd like to know that she's all right."

"No problem. Now, would you like to hear about our adventures out in Ballinasloe?"

"Yes please," the group said.

Flynn told the story of the discovery of the secret room at the builder's yard, and what it contained.

"OK, so we have Sweeney Senior nicely connected to the forged money. That must please you, Paul?" Lyons said.

"Well, let's not count our chickens, Inspector. We have to wait until forensics can make sense of it all, but it certainly looks promising."

"Speaking of forensics, has anyone heard from Sinéad this afternoon? I was expecting her to confirm a few things for us."

"No, not a word," Flynn said.

"OK. Well, I'll give her a call when we are finished here. I don't think there's a lot more we can do till we hear back from her. Our two guests will just have to wait till the morning for our attention. I'll get Mick to extend their stay with us to 48 hours to give us a bit of time to get things sorted. But right now, I think that's all we can do, unless you have anything for us, John?"

"'fraid not, boss. I'm still waiting for the bank in Utrecht to get back to me. I have asked them for details of the source of the funds in Ann Sweeney's account, and they're being a bit slow," O'Connor said.

"Nothing new there. If you haven't had any good of them by this time tomorrow, let me know, and I'll bring a bit of pressure to bear via our colleagues in Amsterdam," Wallace said.

"Thanks, sir."

"OK. Let's leave it at that for now. See what tomorrow brings. In the morning, Paul, maybe you'd like to have a go at Conan Sweeney over the forged currency. I'll tackle Junior about the shooting. We should have confirmation that the gun matches the one used out in Clifden by then. I'll bring Séan up to date as well. Thanks, everyone," Lyons said, breaking up the meeting.

As the detectives began to disappear, Lyons went into her own office. Her first phone call was to the forensic laboratory where she was told that Sinéad Loughran had already left for the day. Lyons was disappointed. It wasn't like Loughran to leave without providing an update, especially when there was so much at stake.

Feeling rather let down, she called Clifden.

Séan Mulholland was still very much on duty when she got through to him.

"Hello, Séan. We have some news about the Ann Sweeney killing. We had a sort of hostage situation at her son's digs out at Moyola Park this morning. He was holding Sergeant Fahy at gunpoint. But she managed to free herself, and stab yer man at the same time, so we have him in custody as we speak."

"Good God, Maureen. Is the lass OK?"

"Yes, she's fine. She's a bit shook up, but she wasn't hurt. Eamon is going to call her later to make sure she's not too traumatised."

"Good. I'm glad she wasn't hurt. She's a fine bonnie girl, that Sally. But listen – does that mean that the son did it? God, that's hard to believe. The word in the town is that he's a fine fellow altogether. Any idea of motive?"

"No, not yet. We haven't had a chance to interview him yet. He had to go to hospital after Sally was finished with him. But listen, there's more. It seems the father was mixed up in some sort of currency scam as well. We found evidence at his yard out at Ballinasloe, so we have him here too," Lyons said.

"God, you'd never know what's going on these days, would you?"

"Well, I just thought you'd like to know about the developments, Séan, but not a word around the place till we charge somebody, OK?"

"Mum's the word, Maureen. But thanks for letting me know."

Chapter Twenty-nine

Before she left the office, Lyons decided to call Sinéad Loughran on her mobile phone. After three rings, Loughran answered.

"Hi, Sinéad, it's Maureen. Just wondering if you have any news for us? I believe you have knocked off for the day."

"Yeah, right! I don't know who told you that, but I'm still here at the lab slogging it out with all this stuff we collected."

"Oh. I called about fifteen minutes ago, and was told you had left."

"That will be Jeremy, our new work experience lab assistant. He's lovely, but he hasn't a clue. Anyway, I'm here sweating over a hot microscope. And I have a few interesting morsels for you."

"And you're still in the lab, right?"

"Yes, of course."

"OK. I'll pop over if that's OK. And if what you've got is good enough, I'll even buy you a glass of wine," Lyons said.

"Now you're talking. But I think you might want to make that a bottle when you see what I've discovered."

"See you in ten minutes!"

* * *

"Hi, Sinéad, so what's the big reveal?" Lyons said.

"Easy tiger. Don't steal my thunder. Which do you want first, the good news or the totally impossible news?"

"Piss off, Sinéad, just tell me!"

"OK, OK! Well, for starters, the gun that Dónal was holding Sally with is not the gun that killed Ann Sweeney."

"What? You're kidding me," Lyons said.

"Nope. Look here. The cartridge we recovered from the scene out in Clifden shows the firing pin is way over to the right of the percussion cap. The one we took from Moyola when the gun went off shows the firing pin in the dead centre of the cartridge. It's what you'd expect from a top-class gun like a Purdey. And there's more."

"Go on."

"Have a look at these. They are the photos taken from Ann Sweeney's bedroom. I'd like to get a second opinion on them, but judging by the spread of the pellets, I think the gun used may have been a sawn-off. I'll ask one of the ARU guys and see if he says it looks like that too."

"But hold on. There aren't loads of these 20-bore guns around, are there? Surely if you were going tooled up with a sawn-off it's much more likely to be a 12-bore?"

"Yes, of course. But if you were anxious to frame someone… well, see what I mean?" Loughran said.

"Jesus! This thing is doing my head in. But wasn't the cartridge the same brand for both guns?"

"Yes, it was. But there are not many makers of those 20-bore cartridges, so that's probably just a coincidence."

"Hmm... and you know what Mick says about coincidences," Lyons said.

"Or, maybe a very clever killer who was out to frame Dónal Sweeney for his mother's killing."

"Damn! And I thought we had young Sweeney banged to rights for it. Anything else?"

151

"Yes. You may have young Sweeney, as you call him, with a few hard questions to answer anyway."

"Oh, how come?"

"Well, you know that we got a good print off the metal straps that were around the sheets of MDF out at the dad's yard? Well, guess who that belongs to."

"You're joking. Dónal's?"

"The very same."

"Bloody hell, girl. I need alcohol. Now!"

Lyons called Mick Hays on her mobile and arranged for the three of them to meet in An Béal Bocht in the centre of the town in fifteen minutes.

"C'mon. Get your coat, Sinéad. I can't take any more surprises for today."

* * *

They were seated in a quiet spot in the fashionable emporium that they often frequented after a tough day at work. Hays had ordered a bottle of chilled chardonnay for the girls, and he was waiting for his pint of Guinness to settle, enjoying the anticipation of the cool, nutritious drink. Lyons and Loughran appraised the senior man of their recent findings.

"What do you think, Mick? It's a bit of a mess, isn't it?" Lyons said.

"No, I don't agree, Maureen. Thanks to Sinéad here, we have established a number of facts now that may well help to solve this puzzle."

"I can't say I see it, Mick. What do you mean?" Lyons said.

"Well, for starters, we can now tie the young lad into the whole forgery thing. It looks to me as if there is a strong connection between the forged currency and the forged first editions, and from what Sinéad has revealed, it seems the whole family were up to their necks in it."

"OK. But we're still no closer to finding out who killed the woman," Lyons said rather grumpily.

"I'm not sure, Maureen. It's quite possibly a falling out amongst thieves. Or maybe Wallace was right all along. It could have been this Pavel bloke after all."

"Shit, that's all I need. More humble pie for Maureen!"

"Don't be too hard on yourself, love. And from what I hear, you haven't burnt any boats with Paul. What do you think, Sinéad?"

"Oh, I don't know, Mick. I just piece together bits and pieces of evidence. It's you guys that have to try and figure it out. But don't you always say 'follow the money'?"

"Good point. And there's someone else you shouldn't ignore in this whole thing too," Hays said.

"Oh. Who's that?" Lyons asked.

"The library lady. I know she doesn't appear to be heavily involved, but she may have had a bigger part to play than the evidence suggests just now. I'd be looking into her background a bit," Hays said.

"Hmm... you could be right. And I like the bit about the money trail. I'll get John to get hold of Conan Sweeney's records and we'll see what we can find out about Angela McCabe too. I might let Séan loose on her."

"Can I make another suggestion, Maureen?" Sinéad Loughran said.

"Sure."

"Could we get an inventory of all the licensed 20-bore shotguns in the area? Say, Galway, Mayo, Sligo, Limerick and Clare. There can't be that many. And then we can see if any have gone missing of late or been lost."

"Good idea. But that'll be a lot of work for someone. There's no central register yet. So, we'll have to contact all the Garda stations individually and ask them to check."

"Maybe Paul could get us a few extra officers. Now that Pavel is back on the suspect list, he may be enticed to do a lot more digging. If you like, I'll ask him in the morning. It might sound better coming from me," Hays said.

"Would you, Mick? That would be great. But I'm still SIO, right?" Lyons said.

"Of course. I'm just lending a hand. It's your case."

Sinéad Loughran observed the interaction between Hays and Lyons with interest. She could see the way their work and personal relationship worked now, but she was damned if she could figure out *how*.

Hays drained his pint of stout and said, "Well, I'm heading home now. I'll leave you to finish off the wine. Can you get a cab, Maureen, and I'll drive you in tomorrow morning?"

"Yes, thanks, hun. I won't be long. See you later."

Lyons offered her cheek and Hays gave her a quick peck, turned and was gone.

"You two are great," Loughran said.

"How do you mean?"

"I can't put my finger on it, but you've got something pretty special going on there."

"I know. I'm the same. I haven't a clue why it works so well, but it does," Lyons said.

"Do you ever fight?"

"Course. But nothing serious, and making up after is amazing!"

They both laughed out loud.

Chapter Thirty

Things were quite intense the following morning in Mill Street Garda station. There was a lot to do, and Lyons was in early to get things moving.

"Paul, I'm sure you want to get busy interviewing Conan Sweeney. But I wonder if you could help us out with some manpower before you get started? We need to try and track down all the 20-bore shotguns in the area," Lyons said when they got together for the morning meeting.

"Yes, sure. Superintendent Hays has already been on to me. I'll lend you Ciara to begin with, and then I'll see if I can get another two officers down later on to give you all a hand. Is John O'Connor going to coordinate efforts?"

"Yes, he knows all the local stations and can point Ciara in the right direction."

"We need someone to dig into Angela McCabe's background a bit too. Maybe see if we can get a peek at her finances, that sort of thing," Lyons said.

"I'll get someone from Dublin onto that straight away. Have we got her home address and PPS number?" Wallace said.

"I have her home address. I made a note of it when I was out there talking to her. It won't be hard to get her other details too," Sally Fahy said.

"Great. Well, when you have that stuff, give it to me and I'll start the ball rolling," Wallace said to Fahy.

"Eamon, I want you to sit in with Paul when he goes to interview Sweeney Senior. OK?"

"Yes, boss. Anything in particular you want me to watch out for?"

"We still don't know who killed Ann Sweeney, so her husband may be in the frame, we just don't know. Don't go straight at him for it, but watch for anything that might give us a clue. When he realises he's up to his backside in the forged currency scam, he may let something slip," Lyons said.

"Do we know who his solicitor is yet?" Wallace asked.

"Yes, it's Lorcan Ryan. He's a very experienced lawyer. We've met him before, and he's no walkover, so we need to be careful," Lyons said.

"What are you going to do, boss?" Flynn said.

"Sally and I are going to tackle Junior. We've got him nicely stitched up for his attack on Sally, so we may be able to use that as leverage to get him to tell us more about his mother's killing. Unless we're very unlucky, he's looking at a three to five year stretch for that prank with the gun, so that may loosen his tongue a bit. OK, everyone, time to get started. Any big revelations, come and get me."

* * *

Lorcan Ryan the solicitor was a man in his forties, immaculately turned out in a charcoal pinstripe suit, smart shirt and silk tie. His black brogues shone brightly, and he appeared to have socks with a pattern of dogs' heads, which Lyons thought a bit blithe given the seriousness of the situation.

When Lyons and Fahy were seated opposite Dónal Sweeney and his lawyer, Ryan opened the conversation.

"My client would like to make a sincere and heartfelt apology for his behaviour with Sergeant Fahy yesterday," Ryan said looking at Sally Fahy. "He was extremely stressed, and quite honestly felt that he was about to be stitched up for his mother's killing, which, of course, he had nothing to do with whatsoever. He hopes you will accept his remorse, Sergeant. Anyway, it's good to see you have come to no real harm," the solicitor said in an effort to mitigate the actions of his client.

"We'll get to that later, but as you know, it's a very serious offense and not one that we take lightly. And it would sound a lot better coming directly from your client, Mr Ryan," Lyons said frostily.

Sweeney said nothing.

"Right, Dónal. I want you to tell me everything you can about this shotgun. Last time we spoke, you told us it had been stolen from your car, which is clearly not the case. Now, we'll have the truth this time please."

Sweeney looked at his brief who nodded slightly.

"I was scared, that's all. My mother has been killed, remember. I thought they might be coming for me next, so I kept the weapon handy."

"Who did you think might be coming for you next, Dónal?" Lyons said.

"Whoever killed her."

"And why did you think that you might be in danger?"

"It stands to reason, doesn't it? Don't forget I lived with her in Clifden till I moved into town at the start of term."

"Were you aware of anything your mother might have been doing that got her killed?" Lyons said.

"What do you mean?"

"Well, she obviously upset someone pretty badly. Do you know anything about that?"

"No, nothing. As far as I knew she was just helping out at the library and doing the odd deal with some rare books. That's all."

Lyons tapped Fahy's foot gently under the table.

"Were you aware that your mother had a bank account in the Netherlands, Dónal?" Fahy said, taking over the questioning.

"That's rubbish. Why would she have a bank account there? She had very little money anyway. Just what Dad gave her and the few bob she got for the work."

"What about the book trading? Didn't that yield a decent amount?"

"I dunno. She never told me. How much was in that bank account in Holland anyway?" the young man said.

Ryan interjected.

"Look, this is all very nice, having a chat about this and that. But are you actually going to charge my client with anything? He's told you he's sorry for what happened. Now can we leave it at that?"

"I'm afraid not, Mr Ryan. We're only getting started. What can you tell us about your father's operation out at Ballinasloe?" Fahy continued.

"He's a builder, isn't he?"

"Yes, obviously, but he has some other business going on out there too, hasn't he?"

Ryan interrupted again.

"Sergeant, if you have questions about Mr Sweeney Senior's business, don't you think you would be better to ask him, and not pester my client in this way?"

Fahy ignored the man.

"Do you ever do any work out there at your father's place, Dónal, helping out, that sort of thing?" Fahy said.

"Not really. I've been there a few times, but he has a good few men working for him. He doesn't need my help."

Lyons took a photograph out from the folder she had carried into the room at the start of the interview.

"So how do you explain this then, Dónal?" she said passing the photo across the table.

Ryan leaned in to look at the picture.

"What's that supposed to be?" the solicitor said to Lyons.

"That, Mr Ryan, is a fingerprint taken from the straps that were used to secure a stack of MDF sheets at the builder's yard. It has been identified as belonging to your client."

"And I presume you had a warrant to obtain this, Inspector?"

"It was obtained perfectly legally, have no fear. Now, I'd like your client to explain how it got there, if that's not too much trouble."

Ryan looked at Dónal Sweeney.

"I don't know, do I? I must have handled it at some point. It's hardly a crime, is it?"

"When were you last at your father's yard, Dónal?"

"Eh... it must have been at the start of the summer. Yes, that's right, probably early July, a few months back."

"That's interesting, because that particular stack of timber was only delivered quite recently. So how did your fingerprint get on it?"

"Look, Inspector, I thought we were here to talk about that unfortunate incident yesterday at Moyola Park. I can't see the relevance of this line of questioning, and to be honest, it's becoming quite tiresome. May I suggest a short break – say half an hour?"

"Very well. But this isn't going away. I'm looking for some answers, and you'll be remaining here till I get them."

Fahy and Lyons stood up and left the room.

Outside, as they walked back to Lyons' office, Fahy said, "How do you think it's going?"

"He's a pretty cool customer. I think we need to up the ante a bit. When we go back in, I'm going to go a bit crazy, so just bear with me, OK?" Lyons said.

"Yeah sure, boss. But first, let's get some coffee!"

Chapter Thirty-one

Conan Sweeney had equipped himself with another solicitor from the same firm as Lorcan Ryan. Gerald Staunton was probably in his very late fifties or early sixties, but was wearing well. Like his colleague, he was nicely turned out, with a tanned complexion beneath a good shock of silver hair which was neatly cut. He was a well-built man, neither fat nor podgy, but his broad shoulders and substantial frame allowed him to carry a little extra weight more or less unnoticed, helped by his extremely well-cut suit.

Flynn and Wallace began their interview with Conan Sweeney in a separate room from where his son was being questioned.

"May I ask what the purpose of this interview is, Inspector?" Staunton said when they were all seated.

"As you are no doubt aware, Mr Staunton, your client's wife recently met with a violent death. And during follow up investigations, we have come across some other matters that are of interest to us, so we will be asking your client questions about a variety of things," Wallace said.

"I hope you're not suggesting that my client had anything to do with his wife's tragic death, are you?"

"Let's see where our questioning gets us, shall we? Now, I'd like to get started, if it's all the same to you."

Staunton didn't reply.

"Mr Sweeney, when we conducted an examination of your premises in Ballinasloe, we came across evidence of forged banknotes. What can you tell us about that?" Wallace said, getting right to the heart of the matter.

Sweeney was taken aback by the suddenness of the question, but recovered quickly.

"I don't know what you're talking about," Sweeney said.

"Really, Inspector, I thought we were here to talk about the unfortunate demise of Mr Sweeney's wife," Staunton said.

"Well, OK, let's talk about that then," Wallace said, keen to upset the equilibrium further.

"My client knows nothing of this distressing matter, Inspector, as you well know," Staunton said.

Wallace could see that the solicitor was getting a little hot, with small beads of perspiration starting to form on his forehead.

"And while we are at it, what about this business with the 20-bore shotgun? We haven't had a sensible explanation about that either. Just lots of stories that don't quite add up," Flynn said.

It was clear that this line of questioning was seriously rattling both men, so Wallace pressed on.

"Let's focus on the forged currency for now, shall we? We found evidence of a large quantity of forged €50 notes on your premises, and we also recovered a fingerprint from the metal straps that were used to secure the stack of MDF sheets. How do you explain that, Mr Sweeney?"

"We buy that stuff as job lots of leftovers. It's much cheaper that way, so I have no clue as to where it may have been before we took delivery of it, or what it may have been used for."

"It didn't look like second-hand material to me," Flynn said, "it was in pristine condition, and in any case, it wouldn't have been strapped like that if it were just some casual leftovers. And, of course, there's the little matter of the offcuts of paper that we found too."

Staunton glanced at his client, and they exchanged a somewhat worried look.

"What offcuts? What are you talking about?"

"In the secret room at the back of one of your buildings, Mr Sweeney, we found bags of paper trimmings. The kind of paper that is used to print currency. And there was, as you know, an industrial grade guillotine there too. How do you explain that?" Wallace said.

"Really, officer, secret rooms; offcuts. My goodness, what on earth are you on about?" Staunton said. He went on, "Look, Inspector, if you have any sensible questions to ask my client then of course he will be pleased to answer them. But if not, I think we will call it a day. Mr Sweeney is not, after all, under arrest, is he?"

Flynn and Wallace looked at each other.

"Why don't we take a short break, Mr Staunton. Let's say fifteen minutes. We'll be back then."

The two of them got up and left the room. When they were out of earshot, Flynn said, "Are we going to have to release him?"

"Yes, I guess so. Everything we have is just circumstantial for now. I know it looks bad for him, but we haven't got any real evidence that links him directly to the equipment we found. We need more time to dig a little deeper into Conan Sweeney's affairs. I wonder how John is getting on trawling through his finances," Wallace said.

"If he'd found anything startling, he would have come and let us know. I reckon yer man has been pretty careful, but that doesn't mean he hasn't slipped up somewhere along the line. Why don't we let him go, and keep a close eye on his movements? Chances are, if he's sufficiently spooked, he'll do something daft," Flynn said.

"Yes, you're right. I'll just go and check with Inspector Lyons that Dónal hasn't given us anything we could use to hold the father a bit longer," Wallace said.

"OK. I'll wait here."

* * *

Wallace found Lyons and Fahy upstairs in Lyons' office drinking a well-earned coffee.

"How's it going with the son?" he said to the two women.

"Not terribly well. He's lying through his teeth. Inspector Lyons has caught him out on a couple of things, but there's been no big reveal. Not yet anyway. What about the father?"

"Not much there either, I'm afraid. We're going to have to release him. There's no doubt he's been at it, but a judge would laugh at us if we charged him just now. And that bloody solicitor isn't helping much. Has John got anything?" Wallace said.

"I'm not sure. I haven't spoken to him. We're just taking a short break before we go back in," Lyons said.

"OK, well I'd better get back to daddy too. Chat later."

Wallace went out into the open plan where John O'Connor was, as usual, focused on his PC.

"Anything, John?" the inspector said.

"I'm just going through Sweeney's bank accounts now, sir. That's the father, not young Dónal. There's a few odd things popping up, but it will take me a while yet to get to the bottom of it."

"Such as?"

"Well, why would an Irish builder have financial transactions with a good few European companies for starters? There are payments going both ways. I'll have to see if I can match them to invoices or records in Sweeney's accounts," O'Connor said.

"Where are these companies, John?"

163

"The Netherlands, Germany and even Poland, and they are for quite beefy amounts too. I'll keep at it, if that's OK?"

"Yes, please do. I'll talk to my people in Dublin too and see if they have dug up anything on the library woman, though I'm not too hopeful."

"Oh, right. Talk later then."

* * *

Lyons and Fahy went back in to continue the interview with Dónal Sweeney. They had no idea what discussion had taken place between the lad and his solicitor during their absence, but Sweeney was looking quite frazzled, and less confident than earlier.

The two detectives sat down, and Lyons restarted the tape machine and recited the usual introduction.

"Right, Dónal, we have to get on. I'm going to charge you with various crimes associated with the attack on Sergeant Fahy yesterday. We'll start with assaulting a police officer, detaining a person against their will, and I'm going to ask my superintendent if we can upgrade it to attempted murder as the weapon was actually discharged."

"Now, hold on a second, Inspector," Ryan said. "My client has already explained that misunderstanding and has apologised profusely to Sergeant Fahy. You can see that he is greatly distressed following the death of his mother, and that behaviour was completely out of character. Surely you can see that such serious charges would have a further devastating effect on Dónal here. For heaven's sake, show some mercy."

"Mercy! Like he showed to Sergeant Fahy yesterday when she was in fear of her life? I don't think so. And we haven't even got started on the connection with the forged currency. Look, I appreciate that you have the best interests of your client at heart, Mr Ryan, but unless he can come up with some detailed information that will help us to untangle this whole scenario, then I intend to proceed as stated. And he's running out of time."

Ryan shuffled in his seat as Dónal Sweeney looked at him with a desperate expression.

"May I have a few minutes to confer with my client, Inspector?"

"Ten minutes. That's it. And please use the time to convince him that he would be best to come clean about the whole sordid affair. It will all come out in the end anyway. It always does."

Outside, Lyons said to Fahy, "Sally, can you go back in when they're ready? I want to see what's going on upstairs. We need to get ahead of this lot if we're going to crack this."

"Sure, no problem. Catch you later."

Chapter Thirty-two

Séan Mulholland was enjoying a mug of tea and a few chocolate biscuits when the door opened and the local parish priest, Father Muldoon, came into the station.

"Ah, good morning, Father. Lovely morning, isn't it? Would you like a cup of tea? It's freshly made."

"No thanks, Sergeant, you're grand."

Mulholland got up from his seat and walked over to the counter.

"So, what can I be doing for you today then, Father?"

"It's more like what I might be able to do for you, Sergeant," the priest said, producing a plastic bag.

"What have you there for me?" Mulholland said.

"A little surprise, Sergeant. I found this in the church this morning, just left by the rails near the altar. It looks like there's quite a few hundred there," the priest said, opening the bag and displaying a wad of €50 notes.

"God, that's odd, alright. Let's have a look here."

"I know we are always glad to get any donations we can. The maintenance on the church roof is always looking for something, but this doesn't look right. We never get any more than ten or twenty euro at a time these days, and even that's a rarity. So, my guess is that they might be from a robbery or something, so I brought them here," Muldoon said.

"I see what you mean. There was something in one of the bulletins I got from Galway yesterday about forged notes, now that you mention it. I didn't pay it a lot of mind, to be honest, but there could be a connection. I'll give you a receipt for them, and if it turns out to be legitimate, you'll get it back. How's that?"

"Sounds good to me, Séan. And there might even be a reward if it does turn out to be funny money," the priest said, winking at the sergeant.

"Oh, you never know. Now, are you sure you won't have a brew?"

"No, no it's fine. I'd better get on. I have a few house calls to make. Poor Mr Tynan is a bit poorly out the road. I doubt if he'll last much longer."

"Right, so. Well, here's your receipt, and I'll let you know the outcome in due course."

"Thanks, Séan. I'll see you on Saturday evening, as usual."

"Of course, Father."

* * *

Mulholland spent a few minutes musing about the discovery, and then went to consult his paperwork on the matter. As he recalled, a bulletin had been sent around about forged €50 notes, and he thought that somehow, a batch of them had turned up on his doorstep. But of course he couldn't be sure that they were not in fact the real thing, and he had no way of finding out.

"I'd better get this lot off to Galway," he said to himself, still greatly puzzled by the discovery of the money in the church. "It's a good job Father Muldoon is an honest man."

Mulholland dropped the notes, still inside the plastic, into a paper evidence bag with a see-through panel on the front, labelled it, sealed and dated it, and summoned one of his uniformed colleagues to drive the parcel in to Sinéad Loughran's forensic laboratory in Galway City.

When the young Garda had departed, Mulholland called Lyons and told her of the strange occurrence.

"I see, Séan. That's a bit odd all right. Let's see what Sinéad makes of it when it gets here. I'll let you know," she said.

"Thanks, Maureen. Needless to say, Father Muldoon is keen to know too in case it's a genuine donation. He could use it wisely, that's for sure."

* * *

Lyons and Fahy went back in to have another go at Dónal Sweeney, but got nothing more from the young man. The solicitor was alert to any tricks the Gardaí might try on the lad, and after another hour, Lyons decided that she had had enough.

"Right. I am now going to charge your client with assaulting a police officer, detaining a police officer against her will, and endangering life with a loaded weapon. We'll bring him to court later on today and see what the judge makes of it all. But I'm not finished with him yet – not by a long chalk. Our investigations will continue till we get to the bottom of whatever has been going on, mark my words."

"Very well, Inspector. We will of course be applying for bail. I presume you won't object?" Ryan said.

"Let's see how it goes. I'm not happy that your client has been so uncooperative. He clearly knows more than he has told us, so don't hold your breath."

Later in the day, Dónal Sweeney appeared before Judge Meehan, and the charges were read out. Sweeney spoke just to confirm his name, and as soon as he could, Ryan, the solicitor, stood up and applied for bail. He told a story about the lad needing to continue his studies, and that any interruption caused by a remand in custody would be very detrimental to the young man's entire career.

"Inspector?" Meehan said.

"We have no wish to oppose bail, your honour, but would request a number of conditions. We would like the accused to be barred from making any contact of any kind with Sergeant Fahy. We would like him to report twice weekly to the Gardaí here in Galway on days to be agreed, and we would like him to surrender his passport. We are aware that there are foreign connections in this case, and we are concerned that he may try and leave the jurisdiction."

Ryan was on his feet again.

"That's agreeable, your honour."

"Very well. Bail is confirmed on the conditions outlined. You can let my clerk know when you are ready to proceed, Inspector."

And that was it. Dónal Sweeney was allowed to leave the court, pending the preparation of evidence by the Gardaí on the various charges.

Back at the station, Paul Wallace had no choice but to release Sweeney Senior without charge. Wallace told Sweeney that he would in all probability be required to answer further questions at some stage, but that for now, he was free to go. Sweeney and Staunton left the station together.

* * *

Later that afternoon, Lyons called a meeting to assess where exactly they were. She asked Mick Hays to attend as well, as she was frankly baffled as to what to do next.

"Thanks, everyone. I know this is a very frustrating situation, but we need to refocus our efforts on Ann Sweeney's murder. Let's see what developments we have to report, and then I'd like to brainstorm the whole thing and see what we can come up with. John, can I start with you? What have you found out?"

"I've been looking into Conan Sweeney's finances, and the library woman from Clifden, Angela McCabe too.

Inspector Wallace put me in touch with some of his colleagues in Dublin, and we pooled our resources."

"Yes, very well, John, but did you actually find anything?" Lyons said.

"I'm just coming to that. Firstly, Mr Sweeney. His business isn't doing too well. There's a lot of debt attached to it, and his taxes are way behind. But he has a good stash of cash in his personal accounts, of which there are several. And he has a joint account with the deceased too, and it's pretty healthy. The last transaction on that one was two days after she was killed. €1,500 was withdrawn."

"OK. Any idea who withdrew the money?" Fahy asked.

"No, not yet. But we will find out. It just takes a lot of time to get the banks to cooperate."

"What about the library woman?" Flynn asked.

"Very interesting. She has accounts in Clifden, Westport and Dublin. Far too much money in them for someone who just works at the library. And there's something strange too. She withdrew €500 in cash yesterday at the branch in Clifden."

"Hmm, OK. Is that it?"

"Yes, for now. I'm starting to get information back about their phone records, but they are a bit slow coming through. Sergeant Long is trying to speed things up a bit. She has good contacts in the phone companies."

Hays, who had slipped into the room quietly and was standing at the back, asked, "What about the two Sweeneys? Where are we at with them?"

"Junior has been charged with the firearms offence on Sally, sir, and we had to let his father go. Lots of circumstantial, but nothing concrete, and his lawyer is a tough cookie," Lyons said.

"Has Sinéad got anything more for us, boss?" Flynn asked Lyons.

"I don't know. She should by rights be here. John, giver her a call and ask her to come across, will you?"

"Yes, sure."

Chapter Thirty-three

The group remained chattering amongst themselves, postulating this and that, until Sinéad Loughran arrived.

"Hi all, sorry I'm late. Busy, busy," the young forensic scientist said as she breezed into the room.

Everyone said hello, and she took a seat in their midst.

"Sinéad, have you got anything for us? We're getting a bit desperate here," Lyons said.

"Oh, right. Well, I have as it happens. That money that Sergeant Mulholland sent in. It's the real deal. No forgeries there, and there's more. Angela McCabe's fingerprints are on the plastic bag. We took them for the purpose of elimination when Ann Sweeney was found, and they are a match. No doubt."

"And you are sure that the notes are kosher?"

"Positive. No consecutive serial numbers. The numbers match with the dates of issue. All the security on each note checks out too. No, they're genuine."

"Christ! This gets weirder and weirder. Anyone got any ideas?"

Hays side-stepped up along the narrow gap between the chairs to the front of the room.

"Do you mind, Inspector?" he said, looking at Maureen Lyons.

"No, of course not, sir."

"Good afternoon, everyone. I hope I can help you all with this case, which does on the face of it seem to be both complex and puzzling. But maybe, seeing it from a distance, as it were, I may be able to put a slightly different perspective on things," Hays said.

Judging by the silence in the room, he definitely had their full attention.

"It strikes me that all of this is connected. It's too much of a coincidence that there are forged banknotes and forged books involved, and everything seems to lead back in some way to the Netherlands. So, let's try looking at this as one big scam. Does anything spring to mind?"

"Money laundering, with a twist," Paul Wallace said.

"Exactly what I was thinking," Hays said.

"Let's suppose that the real game here is printing dud fifties and getting them out into circulation while cleaning up dirty money at the same time. The books are incidental. Just a cover for what is really going on," Hays said.

"I'm sorry, sir, I don't understand. How would that work?" Sally Fahy said.

"OK. Well, imagine the fake books are just being used to move money around. Ann Sweeney acquires them, probably along with a few legitimate first editions, but 'sells' the fake ones to carefully selected targets who need to get rid of some dirty money – say from drug dealing or the like. She receives payment, quite likely exaggerated amounts worth way more than the books are actually valued at, she takes a commission and then sends the remainder back to Europe to the gangs."

"But where does the funny money come in?"

"Just another part of the scam. The money is printed in Holland, exported to Ireland in among batches of timber where Conan Sweeney receives it, chops it up into the right sizes, and re-distributes it. The notes are of very high quality. Probably good enough to get past banks, especially small sub-offices in places like Clifden where no one is expecting this kind of thing to happen. More of it gets caught up in the fake book wheeze too, and before you know where you are, there's a few million being made in such a way that it's very hard to detect."

"Just one problem," Lyons said.

"Yes?" Hays said.

"Why did Ann Sweeney get killed and by whom?"

"I can see the why easily enough. Like many criminals, she got greedy and started syphoning off sums of money for herself. They couldn't allow that to continue. I'd say she had a few warnings, but it was so easy, she couldn't help herself, so she had to die," Hays said.

"And who do you think killed her?" Lyons said.

"That's the last part of the puzzle. But I can't help feeling that the answer is staring us in the face. Look at the MO. Killed with a shotgun that made us look immediately at the close family. No sign of forced entry at her house, so someone she knew, I'd wager," Hays said.

"So, you think we should rule out Pavel Berisha, Superintendent?" Wallace said.

"Well, maybe and maybe not. It depends if she knew the man well enough to let him into her house in the wee small hours. He could definitely be involved. Have you had any luck finding him?"

"No, none at all. He's vanished. He'll probably show up at some stage, but for now that particular line of enquiry is a dead end," Wallace said.

"What about Angela McCabe, the woman from the library?" Eamon Flynn said.

"Yes. You need to get to talk to her as soon as possible. There's a reason she left that money in the church, and I doubt if it was entirely altruistic," Hays said.

"When we're finished here, I'll get onto Séan and see if she's re-opened the library yet. Maybe we should go out to Clifden this evening to have a chat with her," Lyons said.

"I'll leave that up to you, Inspector. But it might be a good idea."

"So, where does that leave us?"

"Young Dónal is obviously heavily involved in both the forged notes and the book thing. I'd say he might be the weak link. I'm not saying he's responsible for his mother's death. That would be very unusual indeed, and after all it wasn't his gun that was used. But he's got some pretty serious charges mounting up against him. It could be if you put the screws on him, he might break and tell all to try and save himself," Hays said.

"Hmm... I think you could be right. Eamon, maybe you could have another go at him with Paul here tomorrow. See if you can crack him," Lyons said.

"Yes, right, will do, boss."

* * *

The meeting dispersed soon afterwards and Lyons went to her office to call Séan Mulholland. The sergeant was just about to pack up for the day when the call came through.

"Hi, Séan, it's Maureen. Listen, can you confirm Angela McCabe's home address for me?"

"Hang on a minute, I'll look it up and see what we have."

The phone was put down, and Lyons could hear Séan Mulholland rooting around amongst his papers for a few minutes before he came back on the line.

"Hello, Maureen. Yes, here it is. She lives in an apartment down by the harbour next to that new B & B place. Why do you need to know?"

"Thanks, that agrees with what we have. We need to talk to her. Sally and I are going to drive out this evening. It was her who left the €500 in the church. Sinéad confirmed it."

"Good Lord. Are you serious? But hold on a minute. She'll not be at home this evening, Maureen."

"How do you mean?"

"Didn't one of the lads see her getting on the two-thirty bus for Galway earlier on? And she had a suitcase with her and all."

"Bloody hell. What time does that get into the city, Séan?"

"Oh, 'tis well there by now. The bus takes around an hour and three quarters most days, so it will have got in soon after four."

"Right. Thanks, Séan. Talk tomorrow."

Lyons called Sally Fahy into her office.

"McCabe has only left Clifden on the bus and taken a suitcase with her. We need to get an all-points bulletin out for her as a person of interest. And can you send a few lads down to the bus station and see if anyone remembers her, especially if she bought a ticket for anywhere by train or bus? Maybe you'd go with them just in case she's still hanging around."

"OK. Sure, boss. What are you going to do?"

"We're going to get onto the airlines and the ferry operators and see if there's a booking in her name for anywhere. We might just be in time to stop her getting away."

"Do you think she's doing a runner, boss?" Fahy said.

"Damn right I do!"

Chapter Thirty-four

Angela McCabe was running for her life. She hadn't meant to get so deeply involved, or indeed involved at all with the whole dastardly business. As a humble librarian what did she know of money laundering and international crime? It had started simply enough. Just side-lining a few books that came in to the library as bequests and passing them on to Ann Sweeney. OK, so it wasn't strictly above board, but the extra money was handy, and librarians don't earn much. But things had become a bit more complicated as time went by, and when that thug Pavel came calling on her late one night at home, it was starting to get out of control.

She hated him, and all that he was about. He smelled of death, and he had threatened her. Oh yes, he had made it very clear that they owned her too now, as well as the Sweeneys, and she would do as they said, or face the consequences.

Things had gone from bad to worse. More and more demands were being made of her, and she was being asked to do things that she would never have contemplated had she been left on her own.

Then, the last straw. But she had no choice. Her life was in danger. She had to do as they asked, or she would surely be killed. So, reluctantly, she went along with it, and at the same time vowing to somehow extricate herself from this web of deceit, lies and death. Now, as she sat on the coach heading to Dublin Airport, she would soon be rid of the lot of them. She would fly firstly to Amsterdam where she would collect all the money she had deposited there. Then she would move on to Berlin where her brother lived. She would make that journey by train. There was no real border between the Netherlands and Germany, so she would be able to travel safely and undetected. She had enough money to start afresh when she got to Berlin. She would make a new life, and try to forget about the horrors that she had been through.

* * *

When the meeting was over, Lyons asked Sally Fahy to contact the airlines and ferry companies to see if they could find a booking in the name of Angela McCabe anywhere in their systems.

Lyons contacted the Garda station at the airport to get things moving. She spoke to an Inspector Faughnan and asked him to set the wheels in motion to intercept Angela McCabe in the event that she turned up there with the intention of getting on a flight.

"It's quiet enough up at the airport once it gets to nine o'clock, Maureen. There are a few flights still departing, but it's mostly arrivals after that, so if she shows up, we should be able to spot her. What's the situation, anyway?" Faughnan said.

"We think she may be involved in criminal activity here in Galway, or to be more accurate, out in Clifden, so we need to question her."

"Hmm... that's a bit tricky, because if we do arrest her, we can't hold her for very long. I think you'll have to come here to do the interview, otherwise she'll just string it out till time is up, and then vanish."

"I see what you mean. Why don't you give me a call if you manage to apprehend the woman, and I'll make the arrangements to travel through the night? Oh, and I'll need your mobile number too, Inspector."

"Rather you than me, but if that's what you want?" Faughnan said and recited his mobile phone number for Lyons.

"I don't really have much choice, do I?" Lyons said.

As Lyons finished the call with Dublin, Fahy came back into her office.

"Hi, Sally, what's the news?" Lyons said.

"You were right, boss. She's booked on the 10:40 flight with Aer Lingus to Amsterdam, one-way only."

Lyons looked at her watch. It was 9:15.

"Excellent. She'll just be arriving at the airport now, by my guess. I'll call Faughnan back and give him the good news," Lyons said.

* * *

Angela McCabe towed her wheelie suitcase across the footway towards the terminal building. She was all checked in for the flight, but her bag was too big to put in the overhead locker, so she needed to check that in.

Inside the departures area, just three of the Aer Lingus check-in desks were manned, as there was virtually no departing traffic left, except for the single flight to Amsterdam and another to London Gatwick at 10:50.

She approached one of the smartly dressed girls at the check-in and heaved her bag up onto the scales, presenting her ticket, which was on her phone, for the girl to examine.

"I'm afraid your suitcase is over the limit, Ms McCabe. There will be an excess baggage charge to be paid. Let me see, it's twenty-two euro. How would you like to pay?"

McCabe was tired after the long journey, and her temper was short.

"Oh, for God's sake, is the flight full or what?" she snarled at the hapless check-in agent.

"I'm sorry, madam, but the allowance on your ticket is 15kg, and your bag is seven kilos over. I can leave it at €20 if that would help."

Sensing that there might be a melt-down any minute, the check-in agent discreetly pressed the red alarm button that was positioned beneath her desk out of sight. As Angela McCabe rooted in her handbag for her wallet to extract the twenty euros, two airport police officers approached.

"Is everything all right?" the first officer said to the girl in the green uniform.

"Yes, Miss McCabe here is just sorting out an excess baggage fee for me."

"McCabe. Is that Angela McCabe?" the man said addressing the passenger directly.

"Yes. Why? What about it?"

"I'm afraid we are going to have to ask you to come with us, please."

"I can't. I'll miss my flight and there isn't another this evening."

"I'm sorry, but I'm going to have to insist, otherwise I'll have to arrest you."

McCabe turned to the Aer Lingus attendant.

"This is ridiculous. Can't you do something?"

The girl didn't reply.

McCabe then turned back to the policeman.

"What am I supposed to have done anyway? You can't just detain me. I have rights!" she said, her voice rising an octave or two as the seriousness of her position dawned on her.

"Just come along quietly with us, please, madam. We're going over to the Airport Garda station and I'm sure this will all be sorted out quite quickly. You may even make your flight after all."

The other airport police officer retrieved McCabe's case before the conveyor belt had a chance to ingest it, and the three of them set off back to the station where they were met by Inspector Faughnan.

* * *

Lyons' phone rang.

"Hello, Inspector, it's Gerry Faughnan here from the airport. We have Ms McCabe here now. She was heading off to Amsterdam on the last flight of the evening. What do you want me to do?"

"Great. Can you book her in and make her comfortable? I'll set off shortly, and should be with you around midnight, unless you fancy a drive across to Galway, of course?"

"Ah, no, you're grand, but thanks for the offer. I'm a died-in-the-wool Dub, me. I get jumpy when I see green fields and sheep."

Lyons laughed.

"OK. See you later then."

Paul Wallace had heard the goings-on, and came in to Lyons' office too.

"Did I hear correctly, Maureen, that you have detained Angela McCabe at the airport?"

"Yes, we have. Inspector Gerry Faughnan is keeping her warm for us."

"Ah, Gerry. I know him quite well. He's a character, but tough as they come. She'll be in good hands. But listen, I would very much like to be in on the interview with her. Do you think I could tag along?"

"Yes. Of course. I was thinking we might get uniform to drive us, but if you would prefer to drive, that's fine by me. I'm bringing Sally Fahy with me too."

"OK. I'll drive. When do you want to leave?"

"Now would be good."

It was a fine evening as they drove across the country from west to east. The soporific effect of the seemingly endless M6 soon had the officers in the back seat dozing off, but Wallace stayed alert, refusing to succumb to the even rhythm of the vehicle.

When they got to the M50 junction, traffic increased a good bit, and Wallace was happy to have something to provoke his concentration. He then took the M1 exit, and in just a few minutes they were approaching the airport.

Faughnan had stayed on to meet them, even though the hour was late, and when introductions had been completed, he said, "I presume you would like some refreshments after your long drive. It's a bit rudimentary, but I could rustle up some coffee?"

"Thanks, that would be terrific. How is the suspect?"

"Very calm, as it goes. She had a bit of a rant at first about missing her flight and so on, but she's calmed down a lot now. She asked for a solicitor, so the duty man is standing by," Faughnan said as they walked down along the corridors to the makeshift kitchen.

"What's he like, the solicitor I mean?" Fahy asked.

"Why do we always assume that it will be a man? But in this case, you are right, Sergeant. He's the duty solicitor. Young and fairly lightweight in my view."

"Good. Anything else we should know?" Lyons said, taking her cup of hot drink from Faughnan.

"There is as it happens. We went through her case, and we found a diary. Looks quite interesting. Lots of names, addresses and phone numbers, many of them are foreign."

"I'd like to have a look at that, if I may," Paul Wallace said.

"Yes, of course. Take it. It's no use to us. What do you want to do with Ms McCabe?"

"We're going to interview her. Best if Sally and I go in first, Paul, then you can swop places after we've had a good go at her. It may be all 'no comment', but you never know."

"Fine. I'll get busy with the diary, if I could just use one of your computers. Let's see what it tells us."

"Yes, of course, that's no problem," Faughnan said.

Chapter Thirty-five

As soon as Lyons and Fahy stepped into the interview room at the airport Garda station, the young duty solicitor began to protest.

"Really, Inspector, this is quite outrageous. What time of night do you think this is? My client has rights, you know."

"Well then, the sooner we get started, the sooner she'll be able to get on about her business, won't she? Now why don't we all take a seat? We have some questions for Ms McCabe."

"Can you tell us, Ms McCabe, why you were apparently leaving the country in such a hurry tonight?" Fahy asked.

"I was just going for a few days to Amsterdam. A kind of mini-break. There's no law against that, is there?"

"And I presume you had made arrangements with your employers for cover at the Clifden Library for the time that you were going to be away?" Fahy said.

"No comment."

"How come you only had a one-way ticket, Ms McCabe?" Lyons said.

"Sometimes it's cheaper to buy two one-ways than a return. I was going to buy the other half once I got to Amsterdam."

"I see. Tell us about your connections with the Netherlands then," Lyons said.

"I don't have any. It's just a nice place to visit."

"I don't think that's really true, now is it, Angela? You see, we found a notebook in your suitcase with lots of names, addresses and telephone numbers in the Netherlands, so you obviously have connections there."

"No comment."

"What do you know of a man called Pavel Berisha?" Lyons said.

At this McCabe's eyes flared and she looked extremely shaky.

"You may as well tell us, Angela. We'll find out soon enough in any case," Fahy said.

Angela McCabe remained silent for quite a long time. She was obviously contemplating her options. Lyons had seen this many times, and waited patiently for the process to take its own course. After a few more minutes of silence, McCabe issued a long heavy sigh and sat back in her chair.

"All right. I'll tell you," she said.

The solicitor reacted immediately.

"Ms McCabe, I'd strongly advise you to say nothing more at this time."

"No. No, it's time this all came out before someone else is killed or injured."

Lyons looked at Fahy and smiled imperceptibly.

"It all started innocently enough. Ann was working at the library, and I noticed that she took a keen interest in any donations of books that we received. Then I spotted that she was helping herself to one or two of them. It wasn't exactly theft, after all the books didn't cost the library anything, but I was uncomfortable with it. When I questioned her, she said that we could both make some good money, and went on to describe the scheme that she had for trading in rare books. Later she told me that some of them weren't actually old at all, but that she was getting them printed in Holland."

"I see. And did you go along with this scheme, Angela?"

"Yes, I did. I don't earn much as a librarian, and I needed the money, so I started helping her out. Her son, Dónal, was in on it too. He did a lot of the donkey work for her. It was a good wheeze. I made a few thousand from it, and no one was getting hurt, so it was easy to justify."

"But it didn't stop there, Angela, did it?" Lyons said.

The solicitor put his hand on Angela McCabe's arm, but she shrugged it off.

"No, it didn't. After a while, Ann said that her husband was coming in on the business too. She told me about the forged money, and said that he was looking for distributors."

"How did that work?"

"Ann would bring bundles of €50 notes to the library and after hours I would go around the towns out in the west passing some of them in shops, hotels, and even lodging them in banks. Nobody ever suspected that they were forgeries. The Sweeneys seemed to have bank accounts everywhere. I even sent money by Western Union using the forged notes, and no one ever suspected."

"How much passed through your hands?" Lyons said.

"Oh, I don't know. Maybe 50,000 or thereabouts. It was over quite a long period of time."

"I see. So why are you suddenly getting out, and don't give us that crap about a mini-break in Amsterdam?"

"It was all going so well till that foreign guy, Pavel, turned up. He came to the library one day as I was closing up. He was pure evil, that one. His eyes were cold like ice, and he spoke in a menacing tone all the time. I was scared rigid of him."

"What did he want?" Fahy said.

McCabe went quiet again, and this time leaned forwards, her head in her hands, and she started to weep silently.

"I couldn't help it. It was her or me. He made that very clear."

"How do you mean?"

"He told me that Ann was stealing money from them, and they couldn't allow that to happen. They needed to teach the Irish a lesson that you don't mess with them, whoever they actually are. I never really found out. He told me that I had to kill Ann, and if I didn't, he would kill both of us. And then he said that now that I was part of the operation, I would be in it for ever. There was no way to leave. He told me not to think of running, because they would find me wherever in the world I went. It was horrible."

"So, are you saying that you killed Ann Sweeney, Angela?"

McCabe nodded tearfully.

"I wonder if we could take a short break? My client is obviously distressed," the young solicitor said.

"Yes, all right. Say fifteen minutes, and I'll see if we can rustle up a cup of tea," Lyons said.

As soon as they left the interview room, Fahy went off to organise the refreshments, while Lyons sought out Paul Wallace.

"She's confessed to killing Ann Sweeney, Paul. She hasn't told us where she got the gun yet, but we will get that out of her. Your friend Pavel was behind it. He threatened her if she didn't do as she was told. In a way, I can't help feeling sorry for her," Lyons said.

"Christ! Who would have thought? Has she implicated anyone else apart from Berisha?"

"Yes, she has. It seems that Conan and Dónal Sweeney are mixed up in it too. In fact, I'd say their lives might be in danger right now. We still don't know where Berisha is for certain, and by all accounts, he's a dangerous individual."

"OK. I'll get onto Galway. I'll ask Eamon Flynn to have both of them picked up at 6:00 a.m. and brought in for questioning. That'll keep them safe till we get to the bottom of this. Are you going back in to continue the interview?" Wallace said.

"Yes, and when I have finished, I'll be charging her with murder and taking her back to Galway with us. Anything useful in that notebook or on her phone?" Lyons said.

"Definitely. I've already passed on some of it, but it looks like a treasure trove of criminals. It will take a little while to set things up, but we may get to crack this gang wide open in time."

"Nice one. Right, we'd better get back and finish this off."

* * *

"Where did you get the gun, Angela?" Lyons asked when the interview recommenced.

"Berisha gave it to me, and told me to get rid of it as soon as the deed was done."

"And did you do that?"

"No. I hadn't a clue where to dump a thing like that, so I put it in the back of a shelf in the storeroom at the library and placed boxes of books in front of it."

"How did you get into Ann's house?" Fahy asked.

"I had a key. We became good friends over the time she was working at the library. We quite often got together for a bottle of wine and a chat about all that was going on. She was a good friend to me. She gave me a key to her place at one stage when she was going away for a few days so I could water her houseplants and stuff."

"So, just to be clear, you are admitting to killing Ann Sweeney by gunshot, using a weapon given to you by Pavel

187

Berisha in her home in Clifden, and you were acting alone at that time, but under duress. Is that right?"

McCabe nodded, still very tearful.

"Right. Well, I'm going to ask you to accompany us back to Galway where you will be charged and brought before a judge as soon as it can be arranged. Do you understand?"

"Yes. I'm sorry," McCabe said.

* * *

Before they left Dublin Airport, Lyons thanked Faughnan for his assistance. Then she rang Mick Hays to put him in the picture.

"Hi, Mick, it's me," she said to a sleepy voice at the other end of the phone.

"Hi. Jesus! Look at the time. Where are you?"

"I'm at Dublin Airport with Sally and Paul Wallace. We intercepted Angela McCabe trying to make a run for it. She's confessed to killing Ann Sweeney. Did you not get my message?"

"Yes, I mean no. John said something about you going to Dublin, but that's all. Are you OK?" Hays said.

"Yes, fine. A bit tired, but Paul says he's good to drive back, and there will be no traffic at this time of night."

"Well, you mind yourself, Maureen. Now can I get back to sleep?"

"Yes, of course. Sweet dreams!"

"Hmph!"

Chapter Thirty-six

Eamon Flynn got the call from Paul Wallace and set up the early morning visits to Dónal Sweeney in Moyola Park and his father out at his place near Ballinasloe. The timing of the two early morning house calls had been synchronised so that neither would be able to contact the other to invent some story about their involvement in what was turning out to be a major criminal operation.

Flynn went with the team to Moyola Park, leaving the Ballinasloe operation to the locals there.

They arrived at Dónal Sweeney's place at just before six, and Flynn organised the four uniformed Gardaí that he had with him.

"Two of you go around the back, in case he decides to make a run for it. You two, come with me and bring the big red key in case we need it."

When they had given the two uniformed officers time to get into position, Flynn and his two colleagues advanced on the front door. It was exactly six o'clock.

Flynn knocked loudly on the door, thumping the frail wooden structure with his closed fist. After a moment, he shouted, "Police, open up," and thumped again on the door, but there was no response. He nodded to the Garda

189

holding the metal battering ram, and in short order the door was breached to the sound of splintering wood. The young Garda stepped back to allow Flynn to enter the hall.

"Oh, Christ!" Flynn shrieked, as he met with the limp form of Dónal Sweeney hanging by a rope from the bannisters, his feet a good metre off the ground. He scrambled up the stairs, followed by the two uniformed Gardaí, and between them they managed to release the rope from around Dónal's neck and lower him to the floor. But they were too late. The body was cold, and there was no pulse. Dónal Sweeney had been dead for some time.

* * *

Out in Ballinasloe, Sweeney Senior, very much alive, was bundled into the white Garda van, protesting loudly and calling for his solicitor. He knew nothing of the demise of his son at this time, and of course the arresting officers didn't either.

Sweeney continued to protest all the way to Galway, and when he was finally placed in an interview room and told to await both his solicitor and Inspector Eamon Flynn, he finally quietened down.

By this time, Lyons and Fahy, along with Paul Wallace and Angela McCabe, had arrived back at Mill Street. It had been an uneventful journey, with all but the driver sleeping a little fitfully for most of the way. As soon as they got to the station, Flynn took Lyons to her office and told her what they had found out at the student lodgings at Moyola.

"Good God, Eamon. Suicide?"

"We're not sure. There was no note, and no evidence of last-minute grasping at the noose which is usual in these cases. Many of them rip their fingernails off trying to get loose when they start to choke. But it certainly looks self-inflicted. I have Sinéad and her team out there now going over the place. The guy he shares with is in bits. We can talk to him later. How did you get on?"

"Oh, fine. Angela McCabe has confessed to killing Ann Sweeney. She says she was forced into it by this elusive Pavel Berisha bloke. I must say, I'd like a few hours with him on his own in an interview room, but he's probably not even in the country. Sally is charging her now, and we'll get her in front of Judge Meehan later," Lyons said.

"Bail?"

"We'll oppose. After all she was intercepted at the airport trying to leave, and I'll make a case for her own safety too, especially with this morning's events. For all we know, Berisha may have killed Dónal Sweeney," Lyons said.

"That's a bit far-fetched, isn't it?" Flynn said.

"Nothing to do with this case would surprise me, Eamon. Now, let's go and have a chat with Conan. I'm not looking forward to this!"

* * *

Conan Sweeney was in the interview room along with his solicitor Gerald Staunton, who, despite the ungodly hour, was once again immaculately turned out. True to form, as soon as Lyons and Flynn entered the room, he started to protest.

"Really, Inspector, this is too much. You have no right to go crashing into my client's property at some unearthly hour and drag him here. I'll be making a complaint to your superior – who is it now, ah yes, Superintendent Hays, if I'm not mistaken."

"Good luck with that," Lyons said under her breath, making sure the man didn't hear her.

"Mr Sweeney, I'm afraid I have some very bad news for you. Maybe you'd like to sit down. This isn't going to be easy."

Sweeney looked directly at Lyons, fear beginning to show on his pale face.

"I'm sorry to have to tell you that when my officers went to your son's lodgings in Moyola Park this morning at 6 a.m., we found Dónal inside the house hanging from the staircase. Our men did what they could to revive him, but he had been dead for some time, it seems. I'm very sorry."

Sweeney looked back at Lyons ashen-faced, and then turned to Staunton.

"Is this some kind of ghastly trick?" Staunton said.

"No, Mr Staunton, I'm afraid not. Your client's son is dead, and for the moment we are treating it as suspicious. The body has been taken to the morgue for a detailed examination and our forensic team are at the house now collecting evidence," Flynn said.

"You mean, it wasn't suicide?" Sweeney said shakily.

"We don't know yet, Mr Sweeney. All we can say is that Dónal died during the night. We will know more later on."

Staunton was quick to seize what he saw as an opportunity.

"Inspector, I don't know why you have brought my client here this morning, but under the circumstances, don't you think it would only be reasonable to let Mr Sweeney go and grieve for his son?"

"I'm afraid that's not possible just yet, Mr Staunton. New evidence has come to light linking your client to several crimes, and we need to question him," Lyons said.

At that moment, there was a knock at the door and a uniformed Garda entered the room and spoke to Lyons.

"Sorry to interrupt, Inspector, but you are wanted upstairs."

Lyons got up, suspending the interview, and left the room.

Paul Wallace was seated in her office when she got upstairs.

"Yes, Paul. What is it? I'm just starting on Conan Sweeney."

"You'll have to release him," Wallace said.

"What! Not bloody likely. Who says?"

"I can't say, but I will tell you that it has come from the highest authority in the country. He has to be let go, and now."

"I can't – at least not without talking to Mick. He may well be involved in at least one murder and God knows what else."

"OK, well, be quick. I've been told to get him out of here within the next fifteen minutes, or I'll be back in uniform and posted to the Aran Islands."

"Terrific!"

Lyons waited for Paul Wallace to leave the room. She closed over the door and called Mick Hays on his mobile.

"Hi, Mick. It's me. Listen, what the fuck is going on?"

"I know. I've only just heard. Apparently Merrion Street has got involved. And I'm not talking some menial civil servant. This has come from the minister himself."

"Shit! But we have Sweeney banged to rights. Angela McCabe gave us a statement putting him in the thick of it, and now with his son's death he'll be willing to tell all. Surely, we can't just let him go, Mick?" Lyons said.

"Maureen, love, I don't know any more than you do. But I think we'd better do as we are told. This looks to be bigger than both of us, and I don't know about you, but I quite like my job here in Galway."

"Cripes, Mick, after all the work we've put in on this, and it looks like we're just about to crack the whole thing wide open. This isn't funny."

"Well, don't be too disheartened. You've got Angela McCabe for the murder. That's what we set out to do in the first place. Berisha is probably miles away by now. Young Sweeney won't be giving us any more trouble, and… well, we don't know about his father, but I doubt if he's going to have a long and peaceful life ahead of him. What do you say?"

"Bugger, Mick. Sometimes I hate this job." She hung up.

* * *

Back in the interview room, Flynn, Sweeney and Staunton were waiting patiently when Lyons entered.

"You're free to go, Mr Sweeney," she said tersely.

Flynn looked at her in amazement, but Staunton recovered from the surprise quickly.

"Quite right too, and you haven't heard the last of this, Inspector. You have treated my client appallingly!"

"You can collect a complaint form at the front desk on your way out, Mr Staunton. Now, Eamon, we are needed upstairs."

Chapter Thirty-seven

"Inspector, this is Dr Dodd here. Have you got a moment?"

Lyons was still feeling ratty.

"Yes, Doctor, what is it?" she said, uncharacteristically rude to the pathologist.

"That young man you brought in this morning, you know the one you found hanging in his house."

"Yes, of course. What about him?"

"It looks very like suicide to me. We haven't got the tox report back yet, but that would be my initial opinion in any case. I think he had quite a lot of alcohol in his system, which might account for the lack of a last-minute attempt to reverse the process."

"OK, Doc, thanks. Let me know when your report is ready, won't you?"

"Yes, of course."

Lyons then called Sinéad Loughran on her mobile.

"Hi, Sinéad. What's the story out at Dónal Sweeney's place?"

"Just going over the place now with a fine-tooth comb, Maureen. The fact that the place is a dump doesn't help, you know what students are like. But initial feelings are that it was probably self-inflicted. There's no sign of forced entry or anything."

"Don't be too quick to judge, Sinéad. The types we are dealing with here are very professional, and we now know the lad had nothing to do with his mother's death, so I can't see any motive for him to top himself," Lyons said.

"Oh, I see what you mean. But we get a lot of these, you know. Especially young guys. I've seen four or five in the last year alone. It's very tragic. I don't know what's wrong with them, poor buggers."

"OK, well, just bear in mind that there may be forces at work that would want him out of the way. Be thorough. Wait, that's not fair, I know you will be, but you know what I'm saying."

"I hear you, Maureen. Don't worry. If there's anything here to find, we'll get to it."

"Thanks, Sinéad. Talk later."

* * *

Chief Superintendent Finbarr Plunkett was in a dreadful mood when Wallace, Hays, Lyons and Flynn answered his summons.

"Take a seat, folks. I suppose you're looking for an explanation for all of this. Well, I can tell you I'm not best pleased either," the senior man said.

"What exactly can you tell us, Chief?" Hays said.

"Look, Inspector Wallace here may know more than I do at this point. As I understand it, we have a suspect in custody who is being charged with the murder of Ann Sweeney, and during the investigation other matters have been uncovered that should by rights have led to further charges being brought against the Sweeney family. Maybe you'd like to fill in the blanks, Paul," Plunkett said, giving the fraud squad officer a hard stare.

Wallace looked around the group, and started speaking uneasily.

"It's been decided that Conan Sweeney is to be let off the leash, as it were. His every move will be tracked, and we think he'll lead us to the people behind this series of crimes that involves a major forgery ring and God knows what else. This is an international operation involving Europol and several other law enforcement agencies right across Europe. It's a big deal."

"I see. And that gives your lot the right to come onto our patch with your size nines and trample all over our investigation, I suppose?" Plunkett said.

Lyons spoke up.

"To be fair, sir, Inspector Wallace has been very helpful in assisting us with this whole affair. I doubt if we could have got to the bottom of Ann Sweeney's death without his input."

"Hmph. We are supposed to be running a serious and organised crime unit here, Inspector, and this seems to fit quite nicely into that category. Now, we've handed all the glory to someone else. It will make me look like a right fool!" Plunkett said.

"I shouldn't worry about that, Chief Superintendent. My report will ensure that you and your team get full credit for exposing very significant evidence and helping us considerably with the whole affair," Wallace said.

Plunkett calmed down a bit.

"And what about this young fella that you found swinging from the bannisters?" Plunkett said.

"It looks like suicide, but we can't be sure, sir. But so far there's no evidence of further foul play," Eamon Flynn said.

"I want an open verdict from the coroner, then. Can you arrange that at least?" Plunkett said.

"We'll see what can be done, sir," Hays said.

"Right, well now get out of my sight and clear up the remains of this mess. Where's yer man Sweeney headed anyway?"

"We will know later today, sir. As I said, his every move is being watched."

* * *

When Lyons got back to her office, her mood was glum. As soon as she sat down, John O'Connor knocked on the door.

"Got a minute, boss?"

"Yes, of course, John, come in."

"You know you asked me to have a look at the 20-bore shotgun licenses? Well, I've been in touch with every station in the region, and nothing. There's no reports of a gun going missing. But there is something. A couple of weeks ago some foreign bloke went into the shop on the industrial estate and bought a box of 20-bore cartridges. There was a new girl on the counter. She asked him for his firearms certificate, but he made some excuse that he'd left it at home, and being inexperienced, she sold him the ammunition."

"CCTV?"

"Normally, yes, but apparently it wasn't turned on at the time," O'Connor said.

"For fuck's sake, John!" Lyons said.

"I know, I know. What are the chances, eh?"

"It just about sums up this whole thing. Anything else?"

"Yes, but I don't know if it's relevant. I keep an eye on an app on my phone called FlightRadar. It shows aircraft movements over Ireland. About forty minutes ago, a small business jet took off from Galway. That's very unusual unless there's something on like the races."

"Any idea where it was headed?"

"The app said some place in the Netherlands, but after a few minutes they must have changed the flight plan, because it went to N/A. Do you want me to follow it up?"

"No, don't bother. It's just our prime suspect in an international forgery and smuggling ring making his getaway. Why should we care!"

O'Connor didn't quite know how to respond to that, so he excused himself and left the room.

Epilogue

Angela McCabe was brought before Judge Meehan charged with the murder of Ann Sweeney. The Gardaí opposed bail on the basis that the woman was a flight risk, and she was remanded in custody to appear before Meehan again in two weeks' time by video link. After the brief hearing, she was taken away to the remand centre.

Conan Sweeney's business was closed down. His solicitor, Gerald Staunton, was instructed to make a generous payout to his workers, and sell the builder's yard in Ballinasloe which fetched a tidy sum. Sweeney's substantial house remained empty, and started to fall into decay, as properties do that are not well tended.

Pavel Berisha never turned up again. It was considered likely that he had melted into the underworld of some Eastern European country and was unlikely to appear in Galway, or anywhere else in Ireland in the future.

The information that was extracted from Ann Sweeney's computer and the notebook discovered in Angela McCabe's suitcase provided valuable links to the gang behind the forgeries, and the Dutch police made several arrests and subsequent successful prosecutions.

Dónal Sweeney was laid to rest in the graveyard adjacent to the church in Clifden alongside his mother. It was a sombre affair, with just a few mourners from his class in college. Séan Mulholland attended to pay his last respects to them both, accompanied by Bridget O'Toole who had closed the post office for the morning of the funeral. The coroner did indeed record an open verdict with regard to the young man's death, leaving the door open for the investigation to be re-opened should more evidence come to light.

Inspector Paul Wallace and Ciara Long returned to Dublin and continued their work, assisting Europol with the evidence needed to convict those that had been caught.

Chief Superintendent Finbarr Plunkett, with the help of a creative young woman from the Garda Press Office, managed to spin a good story for the media which portrayed his officers in a very good light. The press release talked up the international dimension of the whole affair, fudging the smaller details for 'operational reasons'.

Hays and Lyons, together with Flynn and Fahy, soon got over their disappointment. There were more crimes to be addressed, and thanks to Wallace's favourable report, and Plunkett's triumph with the media, their reputation didn't suffer.

Séan Mulholland reflected long and hard on the events that had taken place in his native town.

"Maybe it's time for me to give it all up," he said to no one in particular one evening when he was seated at the back of his bungalow on the Sky Road, a glass of good Irish whiskey in hand, looking out at the sun setting slowly over Galway Bay. He had still not fully recovered from the shock of finding Ann Sweeney's mutilated body early that morning after he got the call from Bridget O'Toole.

List of Characters

Detective Superintendent Mick Hays – the most senior officer in charge of the detective team in Galway.

Senior Inspector Maureen Lyons – a seasoned detective with some unorthodox methods.

Sally Fahy – a junior detective who works with Lyons.

Eamon Flynn – a detective with a reputation for tenaciousness.

John O'Connor – a junior Garda who loves technology.

Mary Costelloe – a junior officer in the detective team.

Mary Fallon – a recent recruit who runs the Garda station in Roundstone with her colleague.

Pascal Brosnan – the Garda in charge of Roundstone Garda station.

Sergeant Séan Mulholland – runs the Garda station in Clifden effectively, but at his own pace.

Chief Superintendent Finbarr Plunkett – a wily man who is keen to retain and enhance Galway's excellent reputation for crime detection.

Inspector Paul Wallace – an officer from the Fraud Squad in Dublin who finds Connemara more intriguing than he might have suspected.

Sergeant Ciara Long – Paul Wallace's assistant.

Dr Julian Dodd – the state pathologist attached to the force in Galway with a dry sense of humour.

Judge Meehan – the local man who presides over Galway's Courts.

Conan Sweeney – a rough tradesman who has many aspects to his business dealings.

Ann Sweeney – part-time librarian in Clifden with a very keen interest in books.

Bridget O'Toole – runs the post office in Clifden.

Dónal Sweeney – son of Ann and Conan Sweeney.

Todd – Dónal Sweeney's house-sharer.

Sinéad Loughran – a forensic scientist who manages to keep her sense of humour at all times.

Pavel Berisha – a thug from Eastern Europe.

Angela McCabe – the senior librarian in Clifden who has creative ways of supplementing her income.

Martin – Conan Sweeney's workman.

Gerald Staunton – a well-heeled Galway solicitor.

Lorcan Ryan – another efficient Galway solicitor.

Gerard Mayhew – an expert in antiquarian books.

Miranda Tregaron – the librarian at University College Galway.

If you enjoyed this book, please let others know by leaving a quick review on Amazon. Also, if you spot anything untoward in the paperback, get in touch. We strive for the best quality and appreciate reader feedback.

editor@thebookfolks.com

www.thebookfolks.com

BOOKS BY DAVID PEARSON

In this series:

Murder on the Old Bog Road (Book 1)
Murder at the Old Cottage (Book 2)
Murder on the West Coast (Book 3)
Murder at the Pony Show (Book 4)
Murder on Pay Day (Book 5)
Murder in the Air (Book 6)
Murder at the Holiday Home (Book 7)
Murder on the Peninsula (Book 8)
Murder at the Races (Book 9)
Murder in a Safe Haven (Book 10)
Murder in an Irish Bog (Book 11)

In the Dublin Homicides Series:

A Deadly Dividend
A Fatal Liaison
The China Chapter
Lethal in Small Doses

A woman is found in a ditch, murdered. As the list of suspects grows, an Irish town's dirty secrets are exposed. Detective Inspector Mick Hays and DS Maureen Lyons are called in to investigate. But getting the locals to even speak to the police will take some doing. Will they find the killer in their midst?

When a nurse finds a reclusive old man dead in his armchair in his cottage, the local Garda surmise he was the victim of a burglary gone wrong. However, having suffered a violent death and there being no apparent robbery, Irish detectives are not so sure. It will take all their wits and training to track down the killer.

When the Irish police arrive at a road accident, they find evidence of a kidnapping and a murder. Detective Maureen Lyons is in charge of the case but, struggling with self-doubt, when a suspect slips through her fingers she must act fast to save her reputation and crack the case.

A man is found dead during the annual Connemara Pony Show. Panic spreads through the event when it is discovered he was murdered. Detective Maureen Lyons leads the investigation but the powers that be threaten to stonewall the inquiry.

Following a tip-off, Irish police lie in wait for a robbery. But the criminals cleverly evade their grasp. Meanwhile, a body is found beneath a cliff. DCI Mick Hays' chances of promotion will be blown unless he sorts out the mess.

After a wealthy businessman's plane crashes into bogland it is discovered the engine was tampered with. But who out of the three occupants was the intended target? DI Maureen Lyons leads the investigation, which points to shady dealings and an even darker crime.

A local businessman is questioned when a young woman is found dead in his property. His caginess makes him a prime suspect in what is now a murder inquiry. But with no clear motive and no evidence, detectives will have a hard task proving their case. They'll have to follow the money, even if it leads them into danger.

When a body is found on a remote Irish beach, detectives suspect foul play. Their investigation leads them to believe the death is connected to corruption in local government. But rather than have to hunt down the killer, he approaches them. With one idea in mind: revenge.

One of the highlights of Ireland's horseracing calendar is marred when a successful bookmaker is robbed and killed in the restrooms. DI Maureen Lyons investigates but is not banking on a troublemaker emerging from within the police ranks. Her team will have to deal with the shenanigans and catch a killer.

When a body is found on a sailing trip, forensics determine it is a murder victim. DI Maureen Lyons follows the clues to a remote part of Ireland's west coast. But will she be able to outwit the shady bootleggers operating there, and get to the truth of what happened one night in Oyster Bay?

After a body turns up in a bog in a remote part of Ireland, the victim's brother falls under suspicion. After all, there were few others around. But why? There is clearly much more hidden beneath the sodden surface for detectives to unearth.

Made in the USA
Las Vegas, NV
26 August 2021

28921456R00127